All Guns Blazing

Cal Hennessy was on his way to meet up with old friend Billy Dixon at Adobe Walls. The plan was to catch up on each other's news over a beer or three. But before he got there he ran into two dead men and a bunch of blood-hungry Comanches.

Trouble was brewing on the staked plains of Texas and Hennessy, who was no stranger to it, quickly found himself right in the middle of a full-scale Indian war.

But gun-swift though he was, would even he survive the killing to come?

All Guns Blazing

Doug Thorne

A Black Horse Western

ROBERT HALE · LONDON

© Doug Thorne 2008
First published in Great Britain 2008

ISBN 978-0-7090-8661-1

Robert Hale Limited
Clerkenwell House
Clerkenwell Green
London EC1R 0HT

www.halebooks.com

Typeset by
Derek Doyle & Associates, Shaw Heath
Printed and bound in Great Britain by
CPI Antony Rowe, Chippenham, Wiltshire

Special thanks to
Alfred Wallon and David Whitehead
for their contribution to this novel

ONE

Glancing skyward, Cal Hennessy thought, *No doubt about it.* The summer of '74 was going to be a real killer.

The last decent rainfall was already a distant memory, and even those few *tinajas* – natural water-tanks – with which the *Llano Estacado* was occasionally blessed, were slowly but surely drying up. With no clouds to soften the hammer-blow of the sun, the stagnant, sluggish air hanging above the desert fairly quivered with heat.

Drawing his reins together and urging his shaggy grey gelding forward again, he scanned his surroundings once more. The picture hadn't changed all that much in the last few minutes. The desert – what Anglos like himself called the Staked Plains – stretched away to every point of the compass in a seemingly endless sea of burned-out grass cut through with vast stretches of loose sand. The only relief came from the occasional stand of cottonwood or juniper and, of course, the stunted, ever-present mesquite, flowering for the second time in as many months now that summer was really getting into its stride.

Hennessy himself was as tough as his surroundings:

tall and brawny, with a thatch of wheat-coloured hair that fell to the collar of his buckskin shirt. He wore the shirt outside his pants and pulled in tight at the waist by a soft leather weapons belt. The pants – riveted blue-jeans, tucked into quilled, knee-high moccasins with rawhide soles – were patched and snug-fitting, and the stiffened, broad-brimmed hat which now threw his square, tanned face into shadow, had long-since faded to a pale shade of its original black.

His weapons, by contrast – a Colt .45 holstered at his right hip and a sheathed ten-inch bowie knife sitting at his left, plus a Winchester .44/.40 in a scabbard buckled to his McClellan saddle – were clean and well-maintained. But this would come as no surprise to anyone who knew him, for Hennessy's guns were the tools of his trade, and he treated them like best friends because they'd saved his life more times than one.

In fact, he told himself suddenly, it could very well be that they were about to save him again.

A dozen or so buzzards were wheeling through the otherwise empty sky a quarter-mile ahead, dropping ever lower towards the ragged slash of a winding arroyo that cut through the desert floor like an open wound.

Instinctively his right hand dropped towards the .45, for in his experience, buzzards usually meant trouble: that it had happened recently, was about to happen or was happening right this minute. And Hennessy, an adventurer by profession, had a habit of running into trouble with disturbing frequency.

As he drew closer to the steep-sided watercourse – which was dry as a bone at this time of year, of course, just like the rest of this Godforsaken wilderness – the buzzards landed out of sight and began to chatter among themselves in their raucous croak and caw.

He looked to left and right, ahead and behind, wondering if trouble would come in the shape of Comanche or Kiowa or both. He had friends among the *Nermernuh*, as the Comanches called themselves, but he had enemies as well. And ever since the whites had started breaking the Medicine Lodge Treaty of '67 with increasing regularity, tensions in and around these parts had been running steadily higher.

But everything around the arroyo was quiet save for the cries of the buzzards, as they inspected whatever it was they'd found. Not that there was much comfort in that, necessarily. Hennessy knew all too well that an Indian only ever let you see him if he wanted you to. If not, he could and did remain invisible until the moment he chose to make his move, and most whites didn't know a thing about it till they woke up dead.

Suddenly he tensed and drew rein again. He could smell the faintest remnants of a campfire on the air. No, he corrected himself almost immediately, not a campfire. Something more sinister than that. . . .

A moment later he reached the lip of the arroyo and saw the blackened, still-smouldering skeleton of a burned-out Murphy wagon directly below: that, and the two fly-covered dead men sprawled beside it, being approached now by the buzzards who, true to form, were figuring to start the feast with their victims' eyes.

Although he could have sent the birds on their way with a single shot skyward, he knew better than to advertise his presence in the vicinity. Instead, he found a spot nearby where the arroyo wall had caved in on itself and urged the gelding down into the gully itself, and his arrival alone was sufficient to scatter the feasting flies and send the buzzards back into the air with an indignant flapping of tousled wings.

Up close, the stink of burnt flesh turned his stomach, and he had to swallow hard to keep from losing his meagre breakfast as he ran his ice-blue eyes across the scene before him. The wagon was standing on its nose against the nearside wall, its two-horse team lying crumpled and very dead beneath it. It looked as if the wagon had accidentally tipped into the arroyo, killing the team, splintering the front half of the box and leaving its two passengers afoot and most likely injured.

What was left of the dead men's clothes identified them as buffalo hunters, most probably from Adobe Walls, an ancient Spanish stockade not far from here, which men in their line had recently turned into an unofficial fur-trading settlement.

Neither did it take much imagination to work out what had led to the tragedy. As he figured it, the wagon had been travelling at speed, its occupants throwing caution to the wind in their determination to outrun whoever was pursuing them. Unfortunately, they'd run themselves right into the arroyo instead, and after that they'd had no place else to go.

The state of the dead men left him in no doubt as to just whom those pursuers had been. Comanches. Kwahadi Comanches, if he read the sign correctly. They were masters when it came to making their enemies suffer, and what had happened here proved it beyond all doubt.

He dismounted and tied his skittish horse to the blackened remains of a ruined wagon-hoop, then took a closer look around. The wagon's charred side-boards were still warm to the touch, which told him that the slaughter had taken place earlier that day, maybe a little after sun-up. The Comanches had scalped the first of the hide men while he was still alive, then set a fire in his belly and settled back to watch while he burned from the inside out. They'd even propped his head up with a couple of rocks so that he could watch along with them. They were considerate like that.

As for the other one—

He was just turning towards the second corpse when it groaned, and he realized that the corpse was actually no such thing: that, incredibly, the man had survived everything the Comanches had done to him and was still alive.

He hurried over and dropped to his knees beside the man, whose bloody, beaten features were now beginning to stir. The Indians had pared off his ears and chopped off his fingers, and Hennessy tried not to look at what they'd done to his crotch any longer than he had to. The man's lips moved, but when no sound emerged, Hennessy leaned closer until he could just about decipher the painful rasp.

'Water. P-please, gimme some water.'

He went back to his horse and fetched his canteen. A moment later he was kneeling beside the dying man again, cradling his head with one hand, holding the canteen to his blood-caked lips with the other. A few precious drops slid down the tortured man's parched throat: more leaked from the corners of his trembling mouth.

The man grimaced then, as a new wave of pain hit him. 'Keep ... keep ridin' ...' he gasped when it subsided. 'W-warn B-Billy an' the others. ...'

'I'll—' began Hennessy, but said no more.

The dying man's eyes rolled up in his head, he shuddered once and was gone.

Hennessy sagged. It was never easy to watch another man die, be he friend, enemy or total stranger. It made him feel powerless, angry and constantly at the mercy of an unkind fate. A few solemn moments passed, and then he got back to his feet and stoppered the canteen.

Billy, he thought, remembering the dead man's final words.

He wondered if that would be Billy Dixon, the old friend he'd come all this way to see.

Little more than a year earlier, Hennessy had hunted buffalo with Billy Dixon, a one-time Army scout and freighter like himself. But now memories of the buffalo stirred painful emotions within him, and with good reason.

Not that many years before, vast herds had roamed the plains. They'd been numbered in the millions back then, maybe even as many as sixty million. But somewhere along the line all that had changed, and where once the magnificent bison – to give it its correct name – had stood proud, free and plentiful, there now lay only stinking carcasses and bleached bones to mark its place . . . and these too were numbered in the millions.

It was an image that gave him no pleasure. Indeed, he still felt guilty about his own part in the decimation of the herds up in Kansas, though he'd heard tell that men like Bill Cody remained happy to boast about killing two thousand buffalo every year all by themselves.

The man who'd just died had killed them as well, and now he'd paid the ultimate price for it. But then, he'd known the risks he was taking. This was Comanche country, after all, a mere fraction of that vast, untamed expanse known as *Comancheria*, and white men had no real business being here and were in fact prohibited by government treaty from plying their bloody trade south of the Arkansas River.

That didn't stop the hide men, though, not when the rewards for such wholesale slaughter were so great. Hennessy had heard that right now, skins alone could fetch three or four dollars each, and while that might not sound like much, it looked a damn' sight more impressive when you multiplied it by Cody's two thousand.

He allowed himself a tired sigh. All was quiet save for the occasional *crack* of overheated wagon boards and the persistent buzzing of flies beyond number. Neither had the buzzards gone far, he noted. But if he had anything to do with it, they wouldn't be feeding on these poor sonsofbitches today. They'd suffered enough, he reckoned, and he felt that a decent burial was the least he could give them.

He turned, intending to tie the canteen back

around his saddle horn and then apply himself to his grim task – but froze instead.

No more than twenty yards away, eight statue-still Kwahadis were sitting their horses silently along the northern rim of the arroyo, rising coppery and impassive towards the steel-blue sky beyond. That they spelled trouble was all too obvious, for they carried bows, lances, hatchets, even the odd pistol or saddle-gun, and had their bronzed faces painted with the reds and blacks of war.

They eyed him coldly for a long, heavy moment, while he in turn wondered how the hell so many could have come upon him so quietly, and whether or not they intended that he should share the same fate as the men he'd been planning to bury.

Briefly he considered reaching for the .45 so that he could at least take a few of them to meet Satan with him. But then it came to him that if the Comanches had wanted to kill him, he'd be dead by now.

That made him think again, and quickly then he tried to remember some of the pidgin Comanche he'd learned and then forgotten twelve months earlier. Cursing his lousy memory, he finally raised his right hand, palm out, and said, '*Haa maruawe.*'

That surprised them, as he'd hoped it would, for whatever else they'd been expecting him to do, they certainly hadn't expected him to greet them in their own uniquely intimidating tongue.

An Indian at the centre of the line said, '*Unha numu techwa eju?*'

Hennessy shook his head and replied haltingly,

'*Niatz. Taibo tekwapu.*'

'*Unha hakai nahniaka?*' asked the Indian.

'*Nu nahnia tsa* Hennessy.'

His frown deepening now, the Indian kicked his spotted pony forward and down into the arroyo, leaving the rest of his men where they were. He, like almost every male Comanche, looked to be short and stocky, with the warped legs of a life-long horseman. He was bare-chested but for a breastplate fashioned out of buffalo bones, and wore fringed leggings. His long, greasy black hair was centre-parted, and framed a copper-coloured face that was flat and round, with deep-set eyes and flared nostrils. It was hard to put an age to him, as it was to so many Indians, but Hennessy figured he must be in his early twenties, a few years younger than Hennessy himself.

As he came closer, Hennessy was surprised to recognize him. Their paths had crossed about a year before, during which time a sort of nodding acquaintanceship had developed between them. His name was ... Hennessy searched for a moment, then had it: Eagle Hand. He was a young brave whose courage was beyond question, but who could sometimes be hot-headed and hasty in his judgments. As Hennessy recalled it, Eagle Hand had later started riding with a Comanche-white half-breed called Quanah Parker.

One look at the Comanche's chiselled face told him that recognition was mutual. Eagle Hand halted his mount no more than four yards away, studied him some more, then said in deep, slow English, 'Hennessy. Is a bad time for you to pass through this country.'

'This I know,' Hennessy replied, also reverting to English. He hooked a thumb over his shoulder at the dead buffalo hunters. 'You have been busy, I see.'

A hard grin touched Eagle Hand's mouth, and he clenched his left hand and shook it forcefully. 'They butcher the buffalo, these whites,' he said, speaking through set teeth. 'They slaughter *P'te* for no other reason than that they *can*. Is it right that we should watch and do nothing, while your people take everything from us?' In answer to his own question, he shook his head. 'You have shared the life of the *Nermernuh*, Hennessy. You above all others should know what *P'te* means to us.'

Hennessy knew, right enough – he knew what the buffalo meant to all the Plains Indians, if it came to that. It meant everything. But this wasn't his fight, and he didn't figure to buy into it.

'I don't want any trouble with you, Eagle Hand,' he said, already starting to regret his decision to head for Adobe Walls at just this time, for no other reason than to shake Billy Dixon's hand once more and recollect their rambunctious past together over a lukewarm beer or three. 'I look upon your cousin, Stormbringer, as a friend, and I see you in the same light.'

'Your friendship with Stormbringer flourished in a different time,' Eagle Hand responded. 'Much has happened since then, and much has come to pass. The great shaman, Isatai, tells us that the time has come to chase your people from this land. That only then will the buffalo return, and everything be as it was in the Shining Times.'

16

Reluctant as he was to get involved, Hennessy had to shake his head when he heard that. 'The Shining Times have gone, Eagle Hand, and will never return,' he pointed out. 'This, I believe, your heart already knows. But know this, too. If you start a war, the blue-coats will come – and come in numbers you can't even begin to imagine – and you will die. Maybe all of you. Is that what you want?'

'This I do *not* want,' Eagle Hand returned. 'But there will be war. This, Isatai has foreseen. Mother Earth will turn upside down and devour you. She will bury you and your miserable hearts, and then peace will return, and *P'te* will once again blacken the earth with his great herds.' He paused, then said, 'Hennessy, I say this to you. Ride away from this place, for if you stay, you too will die with your white brothers.'

Hearing that, Hennessy allowed himself a barely discernible sigh of relief. It wasn't going to come to shooting, then: for old times' sake – if you could call it that – Eagle Hand was going to let him ride free.

Before he could respond, however, one of the Comanches on the rim suddenly cried, '*Niatz!*' and leapt from his pony to scramble down into the arroyo, spilling rocks and kicking up a great cloud of yellow dust as he came.

Even before he reached Eagle Hand, he started chattering and gesturing angrily. He was young, maybe eighteen summers or so, unusually slim for a Comanche but still undeniably powerful. He wore a long breech clout, and had a tomahawk shoved into the red cloth sash that encircled his waist. His long hair was braided in what appeared to be otterskin drops.

Although Hennessy didn't understand the half of it, the Comanche's meaning was plain enough. He didn't think Hennessy should get off so lightly. He was a white man, and the Sacred Powers had decreed that all white men must die. The equally headstrong bucks watching and listening from the ridge nodded and murmured agreement, so it was clear that the young Comanche was speaking for all of them.

Eagle Hand let him have his say, as was the Comanche custom, then raised one hand to silence the onlookers and shook his head. '*Niatz!*' he intoned, much to his companions' displeasure. The decision, he said, was his to make, and he had made it. 'The white man lives,' he pronounced, but added, '*this* time.'

If he'd been hoping to quell any rebellion with that particular concession, however, he was in for a disappointment. The young buck pulled a face, and then, without warning, leapt at Hennessy, lashing out with a brutal backhander that threw him off his feet.

'*Tahkay!*' roared Eagle Hand, his voice all but drowned by the sudden cacophony of approving whoops and catcalls that rose from the Indians on the rim.

But the young buck, Tahkay, paid him no mind. Spurred on by the enthusiastic hoots and hollers of his blood-hungry brothers above, he danced around for a moment, fired up by the prospect of making another kill, then snarled, '*Maywaykin, tzensa!*' and charged at his fallen opponent, moving in a bronzed blur.

Still sprawled breathless on his back, Hennessy

tasted the blood on his lip and fought down a sudden, instinctive flare of anger. That was the last thing he needed right now, because if this Tahkay had anything to do with it, he was going to have to fight after all. And the hell of it was, he daren't do otherwise. The Comanches would take that as a sign of weakness, and if he tried turning the other cheek with these buckos, he'd more than likely get it hacked off.

So he forced himself to stay right where he was until Tahkay was near enough, then finally made his move. He kicked out, catching the buck's leading leg between his two feet, one connecting with his shin, the other hooking around to take him behind the knee, and in almost the same moment he gave a sharp twist and rolled, toppling Tahkay sideways.

The Indian fell clumsily but was back up on his knees almost at once, and this time so was Hennessy. But on the way up, Hennessy had also grabbed a handful of still-warm ashes from beside the wagon, and as he pushed erect he flung them straight into his opponent's face.

Halfway through climbing back to his feet, Tahkay suddenly choked and grabbed at his eyes, but even as he clawed the dust out of them, Hennessy threw himself forward, tackled the Comanche around the waist and sent them both crashing backwards in a heap, with each man trying to punch the life out of the other.

They rolled to left, then right, then back again, washed-out dust rising around them in a smothering haze. Then they fell apart, came back up onto their knees and Tahkay threw a hurried punch that Hennessy dodged more by luck than skill.

Now plastered in dust, Hennessy lurched to his feet and danced back a few paces. Catching a glimpse of his canteen where he'd dropped it in the sand, he quickly snatched it up by the straps and swung it in a short arc. The canteen itself whacked Tahkay on the left ear and sent him staggering sideways, and before he could recover Hennessy swung it back the other way and caught the young Comanche on the jaw, slamming his teeth together hard.

Tahkay lost his footing then, rolled, came back up, scooped up and threw some dust of his own, then started to rip the hatchet from his sash.

Seeing the move through stinging eyes, Hennessy threw the canteen at him and then followed it fast, crowding him before he could pull the weapon free. He hit him again to put him back on his knees, then kneed him in the face, drawing a thick squirt of blood from his nostrils.

Hennessy backed up again then, hoping that would be the end of it, but Tahkay, ornery sonofabuck that he was, still had other ideas. Beside himself with rage now, and seemingly oblivious to the pain of his broken nose, the Comanche swiped at his bloody face with his left hand, more or less sprang back to his feet and threw the hatchet. It turned end over end through the air and Hennessy had to dodge low and to one side to avoid it.

But then it was his turn.

His right hand blurred across his belly and he drew

the bowie from its beaded sheath at his left hip.

The knife was a lethal-looking ten-inch slab of honed steel with a brass hand guard and a bone handle measuring around five inches. As he brought it up and back for throwing, the sun bounced off the blade and a pale, restless oblong of light skittered across Tahkay's twisted face. The young buck's dark eyes went wide, but there was no fear in them, just an almost impossible-to-contain mixture of anger and regret that he couldn't have killed more whites before his own life came to an end.

Hennessy tensed, and was just about to throw the knife and skewer his opponent's heaving chest when his fighting blood suddenly cooled and all at once he wanted no more of hatred and death. Besides, common sense told him that, while the Comanches might approve of the way he had fought, they certainly wouldn't take kindly to watching him kill one of their own.

No: to kill Tahkay now would be to sign his own death warrant.

That being the case, he straightened up, allowed his bunched shoulders to relax, spat more blood and then very deliberately put the knife away.

It was, he hoped, over.

A long, tense moment ticked into history, the sudden silence broken only by the sounds of his and Tahkay's quick, hungry breathing and the occasional stamp of a bored or skittish horse. Then another Comanche dismounted and came charging down into the arroyo, and Hennessy had the damnedest feeling that he was going to have to fight this sonofabitch as well.

But the Indian flung himself down beside Tahkay instead, and quickly inspected the boy's battered face to see for himself the extent of his injuries.

The newcomer was about forty or so, with a thick waist and an old scar that had taken the skin of his right cheek and twisted it into a small, wrinkled spider's-web of dead tissue. For all that, however, the likeness between this man and Tahkay was unmistakable, and explained his obvious concern for the youngster.

Unless Hennessy was very much mistaken, they were father and son.

Glaring at Hennessy now, the scar-faced warrior helped Tahkay to his feet, but Tahkay, both angered and shamed by his beating, quickly shrugged him off and spat defiantly to one side.

Bruised and dishevelled, Hennessy looked from Tahkay to Eagle Hand, the obvious question on his face. Eagle Hand kicked his pony forward until he could look straight down at the white man, then said gravely. 'Get away from here, Hennessy! My brothers wish only to kill every white man they see. For now, I hold them in check – some of them. But for how long? So ride from this place and never return, and be grateful that your friendship with Stormbringer protects you at this time, for it will not do so again.

'Next time, Hennessy, you will *die*!'

TWO

Hennessy's natural instinct was to mount up and get the hell out of there just as fast as he could, but he knew better than to hurry. The Comanches would see that as cowardice, and cowardice was the one trait they despised above all others.

So, eager as he was to skin out right then, he forced himself to bend instead and retrieve his fallen hat, then made a show of using it to brush himself down before retrieving his canteen and finally stepping up to leather.

A long half-minute later he gathered his reins, nodded once to Eagle Hand and rode up out of the arroyo, fighting the urge to glance back over one taut shoulder as the gelding carried him away from the Kwahadis and the results of their grisly handiwork. Only when he was hidden from his enemies by a vast spill of boulders half a mile distant did he finally release a long-held breath and allow himself to sag.

That had been close, he thought. But at least he was still here to tell about it – which he suspected had been Eagle Hand's intention all along. Eagle Hand wanted word of what had happened in the arroyo to spread. He wanted the whites to know that their brief but damaging time here was coming to an end, that he and his brothers were going to wash them away on a tide of blood. And he wanted Hennessy to be the man who carried the message.

Pausing, he checked the position of the sun. It was already well past noon, which meant that he would have to move fast now if he were to reach the relative safety of his destination before nightfall. As if sharing his master's unease, the gelding eagerly picked up the pace.

In the hour before sunset, Hennessy heard the fire-cracker pop of gunshots in the distance and drew rein, but there was neither urgency nor alarm in him now, for this wasn't the furious, irregular shooting that told of some desperate gun-battle. Unless he missed his guess, it was the steady, systematic slaughtering of yet another buffalo herd.

He climbed a high rise from which he could survey the scrubby flats in every direction and, as he topped out, immediately spotted his own particular trail's-end no more than half a mile south-west.

Adobe Walls.

Within the last month or so, the hide men had started working their way down from western Kansas and eastern Colorado in search of easier pickings, and along the way they'd turned this crumbling, long-abandoned stockade into their base of operations. A band of money-hungry merchants from Dodge City had accompanied them, each one figuring to turn a handsome profit by catering to their every need, and the result was this rough-and-ready pocket of civilization in the middle of no-place.

Adobe Walls was a modest scattering of buildings set within four crumbling, half-charred walls built from the clay, straw and water bricks that gave the place its name. To the north-west, a large hide yard shared space with a stable, a store and what he took to be some kind of eatery or mess hall. West stood a log-built blacksmith's shop and a ramshackle, board-and-batten saloon with a sagging shingle roof that looked as if it might collapse at any moment. A way off to the south-west sat a second hide yard, this one about a fourth the size of its companion, beyond which there stood a single, forlorn-looking privy.

Both yards were stacked almost to toppling height with buffalo skins.

The skins brought a frown back to Hennessy's brow. How many were there? he wondered. A thousand? Fifteen hundred? And each one all that remained of a life snuffed out for a handful of dollars.

Before he could think too deeply about it, he was distracted by the sight of two riders coming out of the west, walking their horses either side of a creaking light wagon that was filled to overflowing with yet more slowly-stiffening buffalo skins. Another small group of hunters, escorting a heavily-laden wagon carrying much the same cargo, was heading towards the settlement from the east.

He grimaced as the stench of blood and flayed hides carried to him on the warm air. To the Indians, that same stink would represent a challenge, saying as it did that the whites were here and here to stay, and treaties be damned. For the sorry truth was that these hard-bitten hunters would only leave when they'd slaughtered every last buffalo and left this country much as they'd left the plains of Kansas before it, with Eagle Hand's precious *P'te* all but wiped out.

This time, though, the Indians were going to have something to say about it, and they were going to let their knives, bows, hatchets and trade guns do the talking for them.

It was going to be a bloodbath.

Deciding that he'd tarried long enough, Hennessy touched his heels to the gelding's ribs and came down off the rise, headed for the stockade.

As he drew closer, he noted with a tactician's eye that the largest of the hide yards also appeared to be the sturdiest structure the place had to offer. Although three of its four corners had watchtowers, however, only one was manned, and this by a bespectacled skinner who seemed to be more interested in studying a dog-eared wish-book than the safety – or otherwise – of their potentially hostile surroundings.

He came through the broken walls and slowed to a trot. Few of the grizzled, grease-stained men going about their business between buildings gave him a second glance, and that surprised him. He'd expected the place to be a hive of activity, its occupants eager for news of the outside world, but it seemed that not even the arrival of a dusty newcomer unknown to most of them could disrupt the slow, methodical orderliness of

26

the place, which appeared to be occupied by around thirty or forty men. In fact, the closest he came to a greeting of any kind was when a curly black Newfoundland dog galloped towards him, wagging his tail and letting go a series of deep, happy barks.

Hennessy drew rein and swung down in front of a weather-warped trough that was filled with brackish, cloudy-looking water. As he loosened the cinch and bit to let his horse drink more comfortably, the dog circled and pushed at his legs, determined to get his attention. Admiring the critter's persistence and appreciating its desire to make friends, he scrubbed its big head and ears with his free hand.

When he judged that the gelding had drunk his fill, he tugged on the reins and led the animal towards the saloon, where he planned to slake his own thirst and dull some of the pain in his bruised ribs and back. Still hot from the ride, the gelding went reluctantly, and losing interest in them, the dog trotted back the way it'd come.

Hennessy was just throwing a loop at the hitch-rail out front when the batwings away to his right opened on dried-out leather hinges and a man's voice remarked, loud enough for him to hear, 'Well, I'll be damned! Lookit what the wind's blowed in!'

Turning, he saw three men studying him from the shadows of the saloon doorway, each with a foaming schooner in hand. Two of them – fresh-faced men in their early twenties – were strangers to him. But the third was—

'Billy, you sonofabitch!'

Even as Hennessy recognized him, Billy Dixon came stamping out into the last of the day's light with his free hand thrust ahead of him. Hennessy took it, returning the other's grin as he did so, but there was no shake, as such. Just that simple, firm handclasp alone said it all for men of their calibre.

'Cal Hennessy!' said Billy, his surprised smile all but hidden beneath a flowing moustache the same midnight black as the hair that fell from beneath his tilted slouch hat. 'By God, you're a sight for sore eyes! But what the hell brings you out this way?' Before Hennessy could reply, he narrowed his eyes and asked with comical suspicion, 'Say, I don't owe you any money, do I?'

'Relax,' Hennessy replied mildly. 'Just figured I'd swing by an' say howdy, is all.'

Billy found that funny. He was of a stocky build and average height, and his weathered face played host to a high, broad forehead and dark, good-natured eyes set deep above rounded, bewhiskered cheeks. He, like almost everyone else there, favoured buckskins that had seen better days.

'You're the only man I know who'd cross country like this jus' to say hello!' he chuckled, and he was still chuckling when he turned at the waist and beckoned to his companions. 'Bat! Oscar! Come on over here an' meet Cal Hennessy!'

Billy's friends ambled closer and, while they also gripped with Hennessy, Billy made the introductions. 'Cal, this young grasshopper here is William Barclay Masterson, but he answers best to the name Bat. An' the grey wolf escortin' him calls hisself Oscar Sheppard.'

' 'Boys,' Hennessy said with a nod.

Masterson was dressed for range work in a loose patterned shirt and fringed buckskin leggings. He wore a battered hat with an upturned brim and a well-worn cartridge belt hanging low on his right hip. By rights, his heavy, untrimmed moustache should have aged him, but in fact he looked even younger up close than he had from a distance. His dark, heavy eyebrows sat above well spaced pale blue eyes with very large, very dark pupils, and his mouth had a tight, all-knowing twist to it. Hennessy pegged him at around nineteen or so – but a nineteen-year-old who thought he knew it all.

Oscar Sheppard was a couple or three years older. Thin-faced and clean-shaven, he stood tall and slim in a collarless, sweat-darkened red shirt and creased grey pants held up by a gunbelt buckled high around his waist. As he swept off his wide-brimmed Plainsman hat and offered a shy smile of greeting, Hennessy was surprised to see that he was already bald but for a shadow of fine black hair that grew above his ears and around the back of his head. Hennessy didn't think he'd ever before known a man lose his hair so early in life.

'Heard of you, Mr Hennessy,' Sheppard said politely. 'All of it good.'

' 'Preciate it,' he replied. Almost immediately, however, he turned his attention back to Billy. 'But I reckon I've got bad news for you-all.'

Billy's smile suddenly faded. 'Oh?' he asked carefully.

'Ran into two dead men on the way here.' said Hennessy. 'A bunch of Kwahadis, too.'

'Dead men?' echoed Bat Masterson. 'Hide men?'

' 'Fraid so.'

'What happened?' asked Sheppard.

He gave it to them just as he'd seen it happen, and at the end of it Billy muttered, 'Damn.'

'You know 'em, Billy?' asked Hennessy.

'Sounds like Sam Dudley an' B. J. Williams,' was Billy's reply. 'They went out a little afore first light an' I ain't seen 'em since.' He shook his head and tucked his tongue into one cheek, remembering the dead men and considering exactly what this new development signified. After a while his eyes sharpened again and he growled, almost to himself, 'Well, I guess we'd better go spread the word. Raise a fresh glass to their memories, too, while we're at it.'

Hennessy gave him no argument about that, so they turned and went back into the saloon, a narrow, dingy building with a plank-and-barrel counter running the length of the left-side wall and a lightly sawdusted floor across which had been scattered a handful of rickety tables and upturned crates that doubled for chairs. Too warm, too smoky and none too clean for comfort, the single room was presently occupied by about eight or ten men who were playing cards, shooting the breeze or just washing the dust down with cheap beer or barrelhead whiskey.

Billy led his companions to a spot at the end of the

bar and bought four shots of brave-maker. He tossed his own drink down in one fast swallow, then banged the bottom of his glass against the counter to get the attention of his fellow patrons.

'Listen up, you fellers!' he bawled, and as unshaven, sun-darkened faces turned his way he said, 'I got bad tidin's! 'Pears that Dudley an' Williams ran into some trouble this mornin'. They're dead!'

A moment of heavy, shocked silence followed his announcement. It lasted maybe three seconds. Then, as the news sunk in, a jumble of questions and cusswords rippled through the room, and a bearded giant of a man Hennessy identified as Big Mike Welch stood up from behind a table in the far corner and asked in a low baritone, 'What happened, Billy?'

His question brought an expectant hush back to the room.

Jerking a thumb in Hennessy's direction, Billy said, 'Reckon most of you know Cal Hennessy, if not by sight then for sure by reputation. Well, it was him that found 'em, murdered by Comanches.'

The Comanche word immediately provoked another dark, angry reaction from the assembled hide men.

'They die hard, Hennessy?' growled Mike.

'I haven't seen men die much harder,' Hennessy replied, and quickly swallowed the contents of his own smudged glass to blur the memory.

Caught up in the tension of the moment, Masterson declared excitedly, 'Why, Hennessy had a run-in with the same band! If he hadn't knowed their leader, he'd like to've lost his own hair, too!'

31

Hearing that. Hennessy's lips suddenly tightened and the breath caught in his throat. But it was too late now – the damage had been done. Billy, thinking the same thing, threw him a quick, apologetic glance, then glared at the youngster, doubtless thinking the same as Hennessy – that if Masterson knew as much as he thought he knew, he'd have known better than to tell the rest of the hunters that Hennessy was on friendly terms with the men who'd just killed two of their own.

'Jesus, Dixon,' rasped another of the assembled hunters, a short, big-bellied man who went by the name of Bermuda Carlisle. 'You got some strange friends, ain't you?'

'Bermuda's right!' cried another buffalo hunter, getting to his feet. He was tall and heavy-set, long through leg and arm. He wasn't much more than forty, but his long, straight hair was already bone-white, his full, curly beard only slightly darker. 'If you're so damn' tight with the Comanches, what you doin' here, Hennessy?'

Hennessy recognized him as Hank Ketchum, but just in case he hadn't, Billy was quick to hiss, 'Don't tangle with that sonuver, Cal, just step wide around him. He's strong as an ox an' mean as a sidewinder.'

As if anxious to prove as much, Ketchum took a couple of unsteady paces into the centre of the room, where a single, weathered ridgepole was doing its best to support the sagging roof. His fists bunching at his sides, he rasped, 'Best you drag your sorry ass back to your redskin buddies, mister, 'cause it sure as hell ain't welcome around here!'

He was drunk, or well on the way to being so, and

the drink was making him even more belligerent than usual. But Hennessy had the feeling he wouldn't have been any more sociable, even sober. His longish face was flushed and his green eyes, spiked top and bottom by distinctive white lashes, were glassy and bloodshot. One wrong word, one wrong move, and he'd explode – and all because Masterson hadn't been able to keep his damn' mouth shut.

'I'm not looking for trouble, Hank,' Hennessy told him. 'I've just come from one fight. I don't want another. So just back off.'

'Back off, be damned!' slurred Ketchum.

He was just about to advance on Hennessy when Mike Welch shoved his own table aside and stomped across the dirt floor to intercept him. Mike was a massive man in every respect, closer to seven feet than six, with wide shoulders and a broad chest, a big belly and calloused hands that were only slightly smaller than shovel-blades. His features were overlarge, too. from the heavy brow that hung above his unreadable black-brown eyes down through the broken strawberry of his nose and on to the thick, unsmiling lips that sat above his lantern jaw. He could have been anywhere between thirty and fifty: with his long black hair and full, unkempt beard, it was virtually impossible to say.

'Simmer down, Hank,' advised the giant. 'Sounds like we got trouble enough as it is, without you causin' any more.'

Ketchum glanced up at him and curled his lip. 'Sam Dudley was a friend o' mine,' he pointed out. 'You think I'm gonna welcome a man who breaks bread with the sons who killed him?'

'That's not what the boy said.'

'That's what it sounded like to *me*.'

Big Mike glanced around the room. He saw fear and hatred, dread, excitement and uncertainty in the faces ranged before him, and it was, he knew, a dangerous combination. Finally, he turned his attention back to Billy and said in his slow, ponderous way, 'Comanches declarin' war, you reckon?'

Billy shrugged grimly. 'Sure seems like it.'

'Then we'll oblige 'em,' decided Mike, as if it was really that simple. He saw Hennessy open his mouth to speak but pointedly turned away from him and said a little more briskly, 'Drink up, boys, and call it a day. Seems to me it'll be clear heads that win this fight, and we're none of us likely to think straight with too much of Jimmy Hanrahan's popskull inside us.'

Seeing sense in his words, the other patrons reluctantly drained their glasses and headed for the batwings, muttering to each other about how they were going to teach them Indians a thing or two. Ketchum lingered where he was, still swaying gently, his hooded green eyes fixed on Hennessy. Then, his point made, he headed for the batwings, punched through them and quickly vanished from sight.

Mike Welch waited till he was gone, then crossed over to Billy and the others, leaned his patched elbows on the makeshift counter and fixed Hennessy with a steady look. 'All right,' he said. 'I can see you got somethin' to say. Say it.'

Hennessy sighed. 'The hell with making a fight of it,'

34

he replied after a moment. 'Was I you, I'd just up-stakes and pull out while I still had the chance.'

'Run, you mean?'

'Survive,' corrected Hennessy.

Mike's dark eyes moved a fraction. 'What say you, Billy? Don't set well with me, runnin' from a scrap.'

Billy reached up and scratched the back of his neck. 'Me neither, truth be told. We got some good men here. Push comes to shove, I reckon we'd give them Comanches a lickin'.'

'Damn' right,' agreed Masterson.

Ignoring the youngster, Hennessy asked, 'But why fight if you can avoid it?' He looked from Billy to Mike. 'Every buffalo you men cut down makes the Indians hate you that little bit more, and as of today I reckon you've cut down a right smart of 'em. So, if Eagle Hand's right, and this shaman, Isatai, *is* workin' 'em up for war, they won't hold back much longer. They'll be coming with blood in their eyes and they won't stop till you're gone, the lot of you. Any man with a lick of sense'd be someplace else when they come a-killin'.'

Billy made a scornful gesture with one hand. 'Damn this what's-his-name, this Isatai!' he swore. 'He's just another red trouble-maker, that's all, a dream pedlar.' He shook his head and then, to the surprise of his companions, gave a short laugh. 'Any case,' he said, 'I'll be damned for sure if I ever get scared of a man whose name translates as "coyote dung".'

Masterson chuckled at that, for that was indeed what *isatai* meant in Comanche, but aside from Billy he was the only one.

35

Looking at his friend, Hennessy observed mildly, 'Not like you to treat this kind of business so light, Billy.'

'An' not like you to take it so *serious*,' countered Billy. 'Was a time when you'd whup your weight in wild-cats an' not give it a second thought.'

'That was before I saw what they did to Dudley and Williams.'

As Billy's grin died, Mike Welch crossed his big, beefy arms. 'Well, I think we're frettin' over nothin'',' he concluded. 'The Comanches won't show themselves within a mile of here, an' I'll tell you why. In this here stockade, we got cover. Out there they got nothin'! We've got handguns an' saddle-guns, an' what's more we've got the best of both, an' we know how to use 'em. All they got is bows an' lances.' Using the thick fingers of his left hand to count off the points, he said, 'We got ammunition, we got food, we got water, an' above all we got the guts to see 'em off!'

Put that way, an ill-informed man might decide that it was crazy to worry overmuch about the Comanches, to consider them a poor threat at best. But a man who knew his history would also know that those same Comanches had first attacked Adobe Walls a decade earlier, had burned what was then an important trade centre to the ground and made it look easy.

Besides, Hennessy reminded himself, there was also the Sun Dance to consider.

Although this annual, eight-day religious ceremony was practised by a number of tribes, from the Arapaho and Cree to the Ojibway and Shoshone, this year would mark the first time it had ever been held by the Comanches. Rituals varied from tribe to tribe, but essentially the Sun Dance was an opportunity for the Indians to set their differences aside and pay tribute to the buffalo, their giver of life.

Hennessy felt that his companions were overlooking the potentially worrying significance of the Comanches' sudden desire to take part. The way he saw it, the Sun Dance would be an ideal platform from which they might gain the support of the other tribes, to recruit or otherwise draw them together into one unyielding army united in its hatred of the white man. God knew, the Comanches were a fearsome enough enemy by themselves. But what if you added the Kiowa to their number, the Arapaho, the Cheyenne and others?

Looking into Mike's face, however, into Billy's and those of Masterson and Sheppard, he could see little sense in arguing the point. Their minds were already made up. If it came to a fight at all, they'd fight, simple as that. The only trouble was that, when they were all through fighting, they'd start dying, one after the other, and by then there'd be no stopping it.

'Well, you men got to do what you reckon's right,' he said tiredly.

'That we have,' agreed Mike.

The matter settled – at least as far as he was concerned – the big man nodded 'so long' to the barkeep, Jimmy Hanrahan, then pushed himself away from the bar and headed for the batwings, his movements as slow and measured as ever.

Masterson elbowed Oscar Sheppard in the side and said eagerly, 'Come on. Let's go see what the fellers're fixin' to do.'

As they left, Hennessy shook his head and murmured, 'Lord protect me from greenhorns.'

Billy raised his eyebrows. 'Masterson, you mean?' he asked. 'He's just a kid, I'll grant you, but he's got bark on him, Cal. Came to Dodge just ahead of the railroad a couple years back, got hisself a job layin' track, then decided to try makin' his fortune at buffalo huntin' instead. So don't underestimate him. He's all stay an' no quit. You, though. . . .'

His voice trailed off.

'Me. . . ?' prodded Hennessy.

'You've changed,' Billy said, almost grudgingly. 'You used to be one of *us*, Cal, a hide man an' proud of it. But not any more. Lookin' at you now, I'm not even sure whose side you *are* on. Way you act, a man'd think it's wrong to make a livin' off the buffalo.'

'Maybe it is,' Hennessy replied. 'Maybe I see that now, Billy. Maybe I see that a lot of innocent folks, red and white, are gonna die because of what we've done in the last five-six years.'

'Well,' opined Billy, 'you won't be one of 'em, that's for sure. You've already made your choice. You'll be ridin' on, I 'spect.'

Hennessy nodded. 'First light tomorrow,' he confirmed.

'Then we best get you somethin' to eat,' Billy decided. 'An' then I'll take you over to the barracks an' find you a bunk for the night. There's two empties that

I know of.' And here he shook his head sadly. 'It's for sure that Dudley an' Williams won't have no more use for 'em.'

THREE

Hennessy untied his horse and followed Billy past Tom O'Keefe's smithy and on to the larger of the two hide yards. A stable owned by two Dodge City businessmen named Myers and Leonard had been built against the yard's rear wall, and it was here that Hennessy stowed his gear and made arrangements for the gelding's care.

That done, they headed for the small mess hall next door, which was also owned by Myers and Leonard but run by a married couple name of Olds. William Olds, a chunky man in his late forties, was lighting kerosene lanterns against the coming dusk as they let themselves inside. He wore a creased apron to protect his grey pants and collarless white shirt, but the way Billy told it, it was Olds's wife, a fat woman some older than him, who did all the cooking. According to Billy, she was pretty good at it, too.

They ordered bowls of buffalo stew and when it came, ate largely in silence. At first they had the eatery to themselves, but gradually hungry hide men began arriving in twos and threes, most of them pausing to throw Hennessy a suspicious or otherwise hostile glance before pointedly finding themselves table space as far away as they could get.

Ignoring them, Hennessy concentrated on simply taking the pleats out of his stomach, but couldn't help thinking about what Billy had said earlier. He'd been right, of course: Hennessy *had* changed, and that change, however it had come about, had erected some kind of invisible barrier between them.

Furthermore, now that he really thought about it, his desire to get drunk, swap news and remember the old days seemed almost ridiculous in its naïveté, for no matter how much he might want to, it wasn't always possible for a man to go back and recapture earlier, happier times. Once you started notching up the years, riding different trails and meeting different people with different points of view, life became a sight more complicated than it ever was when you were a know-nothing kid like Masterson, and realizing that now left Hennessy feeling more than a mite dismayed.

When they were done eating, Mrs Olds fetched coffee in a blue enamel pot. She had iron-grey hair knotted behind her head and dark, kind eyes, but because of her size she could only move with effort and her breathing was constantly laboured. As she poured the brew, she wheezed worriedly, 'Is it true what we been hearin', Mr Dixon? That the Comanches're spoilin' for a fight?'

Billy shrugged. 'Looks that way. But if they're fixin' to mix it up with us, they'll find they've bitten off more'n they can chew.'

'I hope so.'

41

Olds himself stopped wiping down rough plank tables and came over to join them. 'There's talk that they've already killed two men,' he said.

'They have,' Billy confirmed with a nod. 'Sam Dudley an' B. J. Williams. But it's like you said – they was jus' two men, an' they was outnumbered by about four to one. The Comanches hit 'em out where there weren't no cover, took 'em by surprise an' didn't give 'em a chance. But things'll be different if they come out this way. They'll know they've been in a fight then.'

Mrs Olds shuddered at the prospect and her husband gave her a comforting squeeze. 'Now, don't take on so,' he murmured solicitously. 'You heard what Mr Dixon jus' said. There's nothing to worry about.'

The woman looked a little less than convinced as she turned and waddled back towards the kitchen, and Hennessy couldn't say that he blamed her.

It had been a long day, he was tired and his earlier fight with Tahkay had left him feeling stiff and sore. Seeing as much for himself, Billy put some coins on the table and suggested they go get him settled in for the night.

As they headed for a long, sod-built structure on the far side of the hide yard, which had been turned into a rough and ready barracks and common room by Adobe Walls's new occupants, the westering sun just started dropping behind the jagged caprock escarpments that fringed this desert country and isolated it from the land beyond. In the deepening grey-red gloom the serrated peaks were a hazy lavender, the craggy shadows with which they were seamed and scored a much darker purple.

Billy took him into the barracks, lit a lamp and then gestured towards the far end of the room, where the plain truckle beds formerly occupied by the two dead men were situated. 'Take your pick,' he invited.

'Thanks.'

But Billy was already turning away. 'See me before you leave tomorrow,' he said, and left the room without another word.

Hennessy watched him go. Billy's manner wasn't cool, exactly, just somehow . . . disappointed, and that gave him the feeling that the last year or so had changed him even more than he knew, that he really was a stranger now to these men and this way of life.

He glanced around the room. He'd slept in worse places over the years, but not by much. The room stank of sweat and urine, and the bunks were packed so tight that a man could hardly squeeze between them to reach his own billet. In a vain attempt to make the place more hospitable, someone had driven hooks and nails into the crudely whitewashed walls at irregular intervals, so that its occupants could hang their shirts and pants up before they went to bed – when they bothered to strip for bed at all, that was.

Hennessy made his choice of cots, took off his gunbelt, rolled it and stuffed it underneath his pillow. Then, tilting his hat down over his face, he stretched out, still favouring his bruises, and waited for sleep.

It didn't come. Instead he saw Eagle Hand's angry face again, saw in the Comanche's dark eyes his absolute, unquestioning belief in Isatai's half-baked

43

prophecies. He saw again what was left of Dudley and Williams, remembered the metallic stench of their blood in the overheated air and—

Thirty minutes later he sat up again, knowing that tired and achy though he was, sleep wasn't going to come any time soon. He listened to the sounds of revelry coming from the saloon, to the noises men made coming and going as if Dudley and Williams had never existed, and shook his head. It seemed that his warning about trouble with the Indians, and Mike Welch's suggestion that they go easy on Jimmy Hanrahan's popskull in order to keep clear heads, had already been forgotten.

He stood up and went outside to get some fresh air. It was full dark now, the scattering of adobes, the tall stacks of buffalo hides and a few parked wagons all sketched silver in the rising moonlight. Immediately he became aware of unseen eyes and glanced up at the watchtower, where a slightly more observant hide man had taken over from his spectacle-wearing companion. Hennessy waved up at him: the hide man barely nodded an acknowledgement.

Thinking back over the events of the day, Hennessy headed north-west on a course that led him behind the smithy and saloon towards the privy, where he took the pressure off his kidneys. He was just starting back towards the hide yard when it happened.

The first he knew was a sudden, low scuffing behind him: someone coming at him in a rush. A split second later something large – a man – slammed into him, caught him a short, sharp punch in the small of the back and sent him crashing forward and down.

He hit the ground on his stomach, the impact waking fresh pain in his already bruised body, but he forced himself to ignore it and quickly rolled to the left, just narrowly avoiding the heavy stamp of a boot that would otherwise have snapped his ribs for sure.

He rolled again, determined to put distance between himself and his attacker, and as he came up onto his knees about a dozen feet away he made out a dim silhouette in the darkness, a tall, heavy-set man in buckskins, with long hair and a full, curly beard.

In almost the same moment he caught a glimpse of the man's hair in the moonlight. It looked to be bone-white. And that was when he realized that Hank Ketchum was figuring to finish the fight he'd been hoping to start earlier, in the saloon.

'You know what I do to Injun-lovers, mister?' asked Ketchum, his voice a low, hate-filled growl in the darkness. 'I break every bone in their lousy, Injun-lovin' bodies, an' then I rip their souls right out through their guts!'

Hennessy climbed back to his feet, feeling his own anger growing and bunching his fists because of it. 'You're drunk,' he said.

'Not so drunk that I can't take *you*,' Ketchum replied, taking a couple of eager paces forward. 'Minute I seen you sneakin' past the saloon jus' now, I says, "Here's your chance, Hank. Here's your chance to even things up for poor ol' Sam." '

Hennessy was seized by a sudden feeling of disbelief. 'You really *are* spoiling for this, aren't you?'

45

The moonlight caught on something else this time – the quick flash of Ketchum's teeth as he grinned like a wolf. 'Oh yeah,' he said in a low rasp.

And then he slid a skinning knife from the sheath at his hip.

Hennessy's gaze was immediately drawn to the blade. It was short, thick and deadly, the bottom edge as sharp as a stropped razor, the upper edge notched by a row of tooth-like serrations that would have little trouble in sawing through bone. As if that wasn't bad enough, the blade ended in a point that then turned back on itself to form a needle-sharp hook, ideal for ripping.

'I'm not armed. Hank,' he pointed out softly.

Hank said, 'Too bad.'

He lunged forward then, his knife-hand thrust ahead of him, and Hennessy quickly lurched backwards, out of reach. Momentum pushed Ketchum on another few paces, but before he could recover Hennessy closed on him fast and grabbed his knife-hand by the wrist.

He brought the wrist down hard on one upraised knee, once, twice, once again, grunting with the effort of trying to break bone, but Ketchum stubbornly refused to drop the weapon, instead swatted him away with a powerful swipe of his left hand.

They circled for a time, each man looking for an opening, until Ketchum made another stab at Hennessy's guts. Hennessy dodged left, avoiding the blow, kept going, came around behind Ketchum, locked one arm around his throat, clamped the other back around the wrist of Ketchum's knife-hand.

Wriggling like an eel, Ketchum tried to elbow him in the belly, but Hennessy tightened his choke-hold and started twisting the knife-hand around so that the hook-ended blade slowly but surely began to turn inward, towards Ketchum's belly. That Hennessy was hoping to skewer him with his own blade was obvious. That Ketchum was determined not to let that happen was equally apparent. But there could be only one winner in this contest, and both men knew it.

Ketchum tried to rake Hennessy's shin with the heel of his right boot. Reacting quickly, Hennessy hooked Ketchum's left leg out from under him instead, and Ketchum went down onto his knees, and under Hennessy's weight nearly plunged forward onto the knife.

Realizing how close he'd come to disaster, the big buffalo hunter suddenly started fighting even harder to break Hennessy's hold and regain the advantage, and now the only sounds were the rasp and saw of their breath and the low, straining, cursing sounds each of them made as he pitted his strength against the other.

Hennessy wasn't having it, though. He was tired and sore and sad and angry, but he had Ketchum right where he wanted him now and wasn't going to let him go.

He drove the knife an inch or so closer to Ketchum's hard-breathing belly. Ketchum clamped his rotten teeth and struggled to push it away, managed to move it by half an inch but no more. Hennessy, his face flushed and sweat-run, forced the knife nearer still, nearer until the needle-sharp blade finally gave Ketchum's buckskin shirt the lightest, deadliest caress.

That was enough for Ketchum. With a roar he half-dropped, half-threw the knife into the darkness, thrust his elbow back again and this time caught Hennessy on the left hip.

Hennessy went backwards, and Ketchum flung himself away, scrambled up off his knees and tried to locate the knife with a hasty scan. Hennessy saw it first and beat him to it, kicked it into some brush and then went back after his opponent.

The blow he aimed at Ketchum's stomach was the kind that would have stopped any other man in his tracks. But Ketchum was bigger, stronger, meaner than any other man, and it didn't even slow him down. With a sudden rush of speed that Hennessy hadn't thought possible, Ketchum crowded him and swung a punch that he couldn't quite dodge. It struck him a grazing blow to the forehead, and he dropped his guard.

Seeing that, Ketchum blurred in and tried to kick him in the crotch, but Hennessy turned sideways on and took the blow on the thigh instead. It hurt like a bitch, but he knew it could have been worse. He shuffle-limped to one side, his leg already starting to numb, and still Ketchum came after him, moving like a runaway freight train. He threw a clubbing left that Hennessy blocked, then managed to land a right to the jaw that rocked Hennessy's head on his shoulders and almost put him back on the ground.

But somehow he stayed on his feet, stayed there and shoved all the hurt to the back of his mind and hit back at him with a jab to the stomach. He followed it with another, another, and suddenly it was Ketchum's turn to do all the retreating again. Hennessy slammed him in the guts a fourth time and Ketchum reeled away, starting to realize that maybe he *was* too drunk to give of his best, that he'd made one hell of a mistake and now he was going to pay for it.

Too bad, Hennessy thought savagely, remembering what Hank had told him just moments earlier.

Again Hennessy hit him in the belly, threw a surprise right that caught the other man on the temple and totally confused him.

Staggering now, Ketchum dropped his guard in order to protect his stomach, but that left his face wide open and Hennessy wasted no time in exploiting the fact. He reached out with his left hand and grabbed a fistful of Ketchum's shaggy grey beard, yanked hard to pull him forward and hit him another solid right that broke a tooth. Ketchum gurgled, spat the fragment out, and Hennessy whacked him with another power-ful right that brought blood from his nose in a crimson cascade.

Two more blows, each one carrying everything Hennessy had in him, and Ketchum was as good as finished. All the life went out of his legs and once again he dropped to his knees, breathing hard – and that was when three deafening rifle-blasts, coming one after the other in quick succession, suddenly echoed from the direction of the watchtower.

As good as finished himself by this time, Hennessy released his grip on Ketchum's beard and the bigger man fell onto his back, spent. He turned at the waist, already stiffening from the beating he'd taken, and looked back towards the hide yard, where the buffalo hunters who'd been making merry were now storming out of the saloon to meet or otherwise confront a single rider who was walking his horse casually through a gap in the crumbling walls. A dog – most likely the Newfoundland Hennessy had made friends with earlier – started barking excitedly.

Hennessy pulled down a steadying breath and carefully checked his ribs. He didn't think anything was broken, but he knew he'd have some lumps to show for tangling with Hank Ketchum, and that he'd better go easy over the next few days or risk making the injuries worse.

Talking of Hank. . . .

He glanced down. The hide man was making feeble attempts to roll onto his side and get back up, but his eyes were crossed and glassy, his mouth working slackly and without sound, and one big hand was swiping ineffectually at the air in front of his face, as if he were trying to swat an imaginary fly. For the time being, at least, he was no longer a threat.

Wincing at the effort, Hennessy limped back the way he'd come, hugging himself to help support his aching ribs and flexing his skinned knuckles to stop the fingers from seizing up altogether. To take his mind off his hurts, he focused his attention on the newcomer, wondering who he was and whether or not he'd brought any fresh news about the Comanches.

The rider angled his horse towards the saloon, but

drew rein before he got there so that the hide men, Billy and Mike Welch prominent among them, could gather around him. Slowing, Hennessy found a place in the deep shadows about a dozen yards away from which he could study the man more closely.

An ill-used Hardee hat threw most of the fellow's lean face into shadow, but what Hennessy could see of it looked to be long, weather-worn and bony, with a pointed jaw across which was sketched a three-day growth of whiskers. The whiskers were the same gunmetal-grey as the dry, straw-like hair that stuck out at odd angles from beneath his hat. Hennessy put him at about fifty or so.

He was loaded for bear, too: that was, heavily-armed and ready to fight. He wore two long-barrelled Army Colts stuffed into the tack belt at his narrow waist and carried a sabre in a scabbard on his left side. There was a .45/.70 Henry repeater in a sheath attached to his saddle and a Spencer carbine in .56 calibre balanced across his lap, its stock decorated with mottled brass tacks.

He slid down off the horse, looking tall and skeletal in his loose homespun shirt and blanket leggings, and deftly untied a large jute bag from around his saddle horn. With a weird cackle he lifted the bag high above his head and gave it a shake, calling, 'Here you go, boys! Full to the brim! Anyone care to take a look an' see how busy ol' Milt's been of late?'

He raised his head a little so that he could rake his gaze across the faces surrounding him, his head moving in short, bird-like movements, all stop, start, stop, start, and when the light from one of the saloon windows caught his eyes, Hennessy almost recoiled. They were a pale, piercing blue, even paler and bluer than Hennessy's own, as if all the colour had been sucked out of them. But more than that, they held a weird kind of restless animation that didn't look quite normal, somehow, and it came to him then that no man would look comfortably into them, for to do so would be to catch a glimpse of complete and utter madness.

'Eh?' the man demanded, breaking his line of thought. 'No takers?' He crowed again, said, 'Then it seems I'll have to show you!'

Tucking the Spencer under his arm, he opened the neck of the bag and up-ended it in one quick motion. Its contents – long tufts of jet-black hair, most of them still connected to blood-encrusted shreds of skin – landed in a heap at his feet.

A shocked hush went through the crowd, and almost as one the assembled men took a quick, disgusted step backwards. In the shadows, Hennessy swallowed hard.

'I caught ten o' them crazy sons, this time out!' the thin-faced man announced, again raking the faces around him with his not-quite-right eyes. 'Ten redskins less, eh, fellers?' He giggled again. 'But they's still plenty work left for ol' Milt yet! Oh, sure, make no mistake 'bout that! Plenty more where these came from!'

That said, he stamped towards the saloon, stepping over the scalps to do so, and the buffalo hunters swiftly opened a path for him, none of them anxious to get in his way or impede his progress, even for a second.

He'd only gone about five paces, however, when he suddenly hauled up sharp, turned and stared hard into the darkness, his free hand automatically moving to the sabre at his hip. How he knew Hennessy was there in the shadows was a mystery, but he knew all right. Even though Hennessy was cloaked in gloom, the other man looked him straight in the face across a distance of more than thirty feet, his wide, bluer-than-blue eyes almost seeming to glow, and Hennessy had no choice but to return his stare and wait to see what happened next.

A long five seconds passed. It seemed much, much longer. Then the other man shrugged his bony shoulders and cracked his face with another loose chuckle that revealed brown stubs of teeth, and a moment later he strode on towards the saloon, the sabre in its scabbard knocking softly against his leg.

It was then that Hennessy realized he'd forgotten to keep breathing. As he started again, the hide men, still watching the newcomer vanish into Hanrahan's, murmured uneasily to each other and began to drift away, none of them eager to follow him back inside.

Alerted by the thin man's reaction, Billy and Mike Welch peered into the shadows, finally spotted Hennessy and headed in his direction. When he was near enough to see the state of Hennessy's face, Billy frowned and started to ask the obvious question, then answered it for himself.

'Ketchum?'

Hennessy nodded.

'Did you—?'

'He's still breathing, if that's what you mean,' Hennessy replied wearily. He indicated the saloon with a thrust of his chin and said, 'Since when did you fellers tolerate scalp-hunters around here?'

'That's Milt Hagerman,' said Billy. 'An' best you walk a mile in his boots before you judge him, Cal. Used to be a sodbuster, had hisself a nice little place jus' north of the Canadian, a wife an' two younkers, too. Then, one day he set out for Dodge, fixin' to buy seed an' stock. That's when the Comanches hit.

'They battered his boys to death, defiled his woman an' slit her throat, killed or ran off his livestock an' then burned his buildin's. If that ain't sufficient to break a man's soul an' shatter his sanity, you'll have to tell me what is.'

Hennessy considered the story. It was an all too common one, and the rest of it wasn't difficult to figure out. 'So he's been killing Comanches ever since?' he guessed.

Billy nodded. 'Just as many as he can, as often as he can.'

'He needs help,' Hennessy said softly.

'Sure he does,' growled Mike. 'But you can't talk to him. No one can. The only thing Milt Hagerman wants to do now is kill every redskin he can lay his hands on – men, women, children – jus' kill 'em and go on killin' 'em till there ain't none left to burn powder on.'

'An' that's another reason the Comanches won't show their painted faces around here,' muttered Billy, a thin, funereal smile finding its way to his lips. ' 'Cause Milt Hagerman scares them even more'n he scares us.'

The tall half-breed with the long blue-black hair stared into the flames of his small fire and listened to the regular, low rumble of drums beyond the tipi's buffalo-hide walls, which were decorated in traditional Comanche fashion with a wild jumble of circles, squares, triangles and oblongs. The erratic rise and fall of orange flames threw dancing shadows across his handsome face.

'What ails you, my brother?' asked a thick-set Kiowa on the far side of the fire. In his mid-forties, he had a round, flat face and slanting eyes above a broad nose, and unlike the man he had just addressed, he wore his hair to collar-length. This was Satanta, also called White Bear, and he had recently jumped the reserva-tion in south-western Oklahoma in order to take part in the Kwahadis' Sun Dance. 'You look troubled.'

'I am always troubled,' Quanah Parker stated quietly.

At that, Satanta glanced uneasily at the tipi's third occupant, who was also Kiowa. After a moment he said quietly, 'This I know. But sometimes you are more so – as now.'

The Kwahadi war chief and spiritual leader didn't reply immediately, for it was important that he choose his words carefully with this man. 'My heart is sad when I think of my people,' he confessed at length. 'Daily I see their bewilderment and despair. They are afraid and they are angry. They wonder where the buffalo have gone and when they will come again, and they look to me for answers. But I have none – none that will bring them any comfort.'

'Then you must find the buffalo,' Satanta advised earnestly, 'or what remains of them. And you must let your people see for themselves how the whites kill him in such numbers not only for his hide and his bones and his tongue, but also in order to deny us all the things we need to survive. More than any number of words, that will give them the answer they seek.'

Quanah considered this with a heavy heart. Satanta spoke the truth, of course. First and foremost, the buffalo was meat, either fresh or dried as pemmican. But he was so much more besides. Without the buffalo there was neither bedding nor fuel. There were no tools, no weapons, no clothing and no medicine, for it was said that the contents of at least one of his two stomachs could fight and sometimes cure disease.

From the buffalo came the thread with which the women sewed, the rope with which the men caught and corralled horses. His hoofs were boiled for glue. His sinews became the strings that fired arrows. and his hide, once hardened. could be fashioned into shields that turned away bullets.

To acquire even some of these necessities elsewhere, the Comanches would have to deal with the white-eyes, and to do that would mean also to observe the white-eyes' laws or suffer the consequences.

Such a course could have only one outcome – war.

Still, that had ever been the way with Satanta. He had always preferred aggression over agreement. In the past he had signed treaties with the whites, but still continued to make war on them until finally they had captured him. At first they had sentenced him to hang, but then changed their minds and told him he must instead spend the remainder of his days in prison. But as was typical of the whites, there had followed yet another change of heart three summers later and they had given him something called *parole* and set him free. He was still a firebrand, though, still one to be treated with the utmost caution, and Quanah never made the mistake of forgetting it.

'If I do this thing,' he returned, 'the hatred that already runs deep within the *Nermernuh* will burn brighter, stronger. They will make war on the whites, and they will die because of it.'

'Quanah,' said the other Kiowa, speaking for the first time. 'You must listen to your people. They starve and they worry. They need guidance, and if they do not get it from you then they will seek it from another. Your own days as leader are short unless you act now!'

Quanah regarded this man thoughtfully. He was Lone Wolf, sometimes called Gu. He had a sloped forehead and a heavy brow, and lips that seemed always to be pinched in disapproval. He wore his raven-black hair in braids.

'Then what must I do?' asked the Kwahadi chieftain.

'You must listen to Isatai,' was Lone Wolf's answer. 'The Prophet is strong and has much wisdom. He tells of a great victory to be had over the whites. That victory could be yours. But you cannot hesitate forever. You must *act*, my brother, and act *now*.'

'This you know, in here,' Satanta added persuasively, striking his chest with a fistful of scarred knuckles.

'That is why you alone refused to sign their treaty those seven summers ago. You showed wisdom then, Quanah, while we showed only folly. My words to you now are to show that wisdom again.'

Quanah nodded.

He was the son of the Comanche war chief Peta Nocona, and grandson of the chieftain and medicine man Iron Jacket. The making of war was in his blood. But he was also the son of a white woman who had once been known as Cynthia Ann Parker, and because of that he was able to see clearly the differences between white man and red, and strive always to make allowances for the failings in both.

Still, war was not without its appeal.

His mother had been captured by the Comanches many years earlier, and eventually lived so long with the *Nermernuh* that she forgot her own tongue and spoke only Comanche.

For almost a quarter-century she had lived the hard, nomadic, self-reliant life of her adopted people. For almost a quarter-century she had known happiness and contentment with her doting giant of a husband and their two sons and one daughter.

But then she had been 'rescued' by those men the whites called Texas Rangers, and separated from her beloved husband and sons, who had been out hunting when the white men struck.

Quanah's expression hardened as he remembered that time.

There was neither happiness nor contentment for his mother after that. Without her man, without her sons, without the hard but free life of the *Nermernuh*, she was broken, and when at last her daughter, Quanah's sister Topsannah, died of fever, she had taken the only course left to her. She had starved herself to death and died the saddest of women, at the age of no more than thirty-eight summers.

Ten years had passed since that day, but Quanah still saw her face and the neat centre-part of her dark, glistening hair, as if the passage of years had been more like the passage of seconds, and still he missed her. He missed her most of all at times like this, when the weight of responsibility was at its heaviest upon him. Were she here now, how would she advise him? What guidance would his father offer, were he not also dead?

The urge to wage war on the whites was strong within him. He had more than enough reason. But he knew it was a war he stood very little chance of winning. The whites were as many as the grains of sand in this *Llano Estacado*. If he killed but one, ten more would come to replace him, and this was a sorry but undeniable truth.

But his companions were right. He would have to make his decision.

He thought again of Isatai. He had no great liking for the man, and even little trust. But just maybe it would be as Satanta and Lone Wolf said. Just maybe Isatai *would* know what to do.

FOUR

The throbbing of the drums grew steadily louder as the three chieftains stepped out into the night. Beneath the cool opalescence of the low-hanging moon, the camp was a close-packed gathering of conical *tipis* that stretched the length of a narrow, unnamed canyon. Here and there, small campfires threw gigantic shadows up across its scrub-studded amber walls, but did little to combat the chilly night air.

Quanah, Satanta and Lone Wolf moved quietly through the camp, gauging the mood of their people as they went. Although this was a ceremony at which old enemies were supposed to forget their differences and celebrate a time of renewal, there was an undeniable feeling of disgruntlement in the air. Warriors and their elaborately-dressed women – not only Comanche and Kiowa, but some Cheyenne as well – seemed to drift from one place to another with neither purpose nor enthusiasm, and even the antics of the 'mud heads' – those masked clowns whose job it was to pass through the camp playing tricks and generally entertaining the crowds – appeared to have no great effect.

Most noticeable of all, however – at least as far as Quanah was concerned – was the air itself. Perhaps as many as a thousand people had gathered for this Sun Dance. The air should have smelled of roasting buffalo and frying elk, of tender antelope and broiled deer, but instead it smelled mostly of wild onions and juniper berries, of roots, persimmons and mulberries, for aside from the odd slaughtered horse, there was little meat here that was truly worth the name.

At last the chieftains came within sight of their destination, a large, circular framework of cottonwood logs over which had been laid walls of close-packed brush, and a floor covered in pure white river sand. This was the Sun Dance Lodge, and it had taken two days to construct. It was here that men would fast throughout the eight-day ritual and then tell of their visions, or inflict pain upon themselves as a means of paying tribute to Mother Earth.

They stopped just short of the Lodge and joined a three-deep crowd who were watching several warriors performing the Buffalo Dance, the purpose of which was to thank the buffalo for the previous year's hunting and ask for good fortune in the hunts still to come. But as Quanah followed each distinctive movement, he found his sadness increasing, for if *P'te* were to vanish, as was beginning to seem ever more likely, then the Comanches might just as well sing their death-chant instead.

About ten minutes later the drums and rattles fell silent, and the dancers backed into the crowd, sweating hard and breathing heavily. As all eyes turned towards the Lodge, into which the shaman, Isatai, had retired several hours earlier, a sudden, palpable sense of expectancy filled the air, for it was known that the medicine man had gone to commune with the gods, and the *Nermernuh* were eager to know what they had told him.

Long, expectant seconds dripped into the past. Somewhere a hungry baby started crying and his mother whispered, '*Shhh. . . .*'

And then the flap hanging over the Lodge's east-facing entrance was flung aside and Isatai himself stepped out into the bracing night air.

In the past it had been said that he looked more like a dead man than most dead men, and this was certainly true. He was tall and emaciated, with thin arms, thin legs, prominent ribs and a flat, almost hollow, stomach. His black eyes were very much alive, though. They *shone* with life, with complete and unshakeable self-belief, and also, Quanah noticed, with a fierce and perhaps unquenchable ambition.

He wore only a black breech clout into which was shoved an ancient percussion pistol, and every inch of his exposed skin had been painted bright yellow save for his face. One half of that was painted in the same intense hue, the other in a deep, all-concealing black.

After a moment he came forward into the firelight, raised his right hand and, quick as thought, flung a fine white powder into the flickering flames. At once a cloud of ochre-coloured smoke burst skyward with a faint pop. Startled and not a little scared, the watching warriors shrank in on themselves, and an uneasy mutter ran through them.

'The Sacred Powers have spoken,' he declared at length. He seemed not to raise his voice, and yet it carried to every corner of the camp, clear and deep, a voice that demanded attention. 'And the news is grave, my brothers,' he continued, 'for the day of the buffalo draws to a close. This I have been told. Daily his numbers grow less, and soon he will be no more. This he knows, and thus he weeps for the passing of his kind. The white-eyes will kill, kill and kill again until there are no buffalo left to kill. And this will come to pass even sooner than we think, unless we act to prevent it!

'My brothers, this I tell you!' he called, his voice now bouncing off the canyon's seamed limestone walls. 'The white man must pay for his actions, for he condemns not only the buffalo, but also the Indian! He slaughters one to kill the other!'

Now the muttering rose to an excited babble, for each man there knew the truth of his words.

'But how do we stop the white man, Isatai?' asked a heavy-set Comanche when the tumult died down. His name was Mow-way, and his flat face was home to high cheekbones and sad lips. 'They are more than we, and better-armed.'

Quanah narrowed his eyes and watched the shaman closely, curious to hear his reply.

Isatai inclined his head slowly. 'This is so,' he allowed. 'But you need not worry, for I shall ride with you into battle and catch every bullet the white man sends against you! I have already spoken of this to the

63

gods, and they have granted my wish – that I protect you all!'

He was expecting his claim to generate another excitable reaction, but when it didn't he looked more critically at the fire-flushed faces surrounding him and asked with what sounded like genuine puzzlement, 'Is it that you did not understand me, or that you did not believe me?'

Continued silence was his only answer.

He shook his head as if in disapproval. 'Then I say again – we shall be invulnerable to the white-eyes' thunder-sticks, and this I shall prove!'

Without warning, he tore the old percussion pistol from his breech clout and once again raked his glittering eyes across his audience. He had them spellbound now, wide-eyed and open-mouthed, completely in his thrall.

'Whoever doubts the word of the Sacred Powers,' he said, 'whoever doubts the word of *Isatai*, is free to take this fire-stick and try to shoot me down! Then he and all of you will see that my skin is made of iron, that the white-eyes' bullets will be useless against us!' He paused, then asked, 'Is there one among you who will challenge the word of the gods?'

There was an uncomfortable shifting and shuffling as warriors glanced self-consciously at each other, Kiowa at Cheyenne, Cheyenne at Comanche, then looked away again. No one moved to take up the challenge.

A brief smile touched Isatai's narrow lips, for he had expected as much. When his eyes finally found those of

Eagle Hand, however, he felt a particular sense of triumph. Eagle Hand was the most devoted of his followers, a warrior who idolized him and made no secret of it. Who better, then, to help him prove his claim?

Pointing to the young brave, Isatai extended the pistol, butt-first. It was an ancient Colt Paterson, a handgun that looked more like a cannon, with a long barrel and a folding trigger. 'Come,' he said.

Eagle Hand looked dumbstruck. He climbed to his feet and shook his head. 'This I cannot do,' he replied. 'If anything were to go wrong—'

'It will not.'

'But if it did, if I were to kill you' – and here his dark, deep-set eyes lowered – 'I would be killing the last hope of our people,' he finished quietly.

The comment was not lost upon Quanah.

'Nothing will happen to me,' Isatai assured the young brave, his tone gentle now, and almost paternal. 'Here, take the fire-stick. Aim well and pull the trigger. The bullet will fall to the ground long before it can harm me. This I say!'

Reluctantly, Eagle Hand came forward and took the gun, judged its weight in his two hands, then backed off a few yards. He looked to left and right, saw face upon face studying him intently, felt his heart pounding against his buffalo-bone breastplate with a force that was almost sickening.

'I am ready, Eagle Hand!' shouted Isatai, planting his feet wide and opening his scrawny arms.

Mouth dry, Eagle Hand raised the gun, holding it in

65

his right hand, cradling the butt in his left, and took aim. The sound he made thumbing back the hammer was harsh and ratchety in the tense near-silence. He looked along the barrel until his eyes met those of the shaman. Isatai nodded almost imperceptibly and smiled at him.

Holding his breath, Eagle Hand took up the first pressure . . .

. . . and fired.

The heavy weapon unloaded with a thunderous roar, bucking in his grip like a desperate, living thing as it discharged acrid smoke towards the sky. Eagle Hand's eyes closed instinctively as he fired, but he opened them again almost immediately, waiting with still-held breath until the last of the smoke finally drifted aside.

He could not believe what he saw.

Isatai stood before him, completely unharmed.

Around them, their audience began chattering in low, awestruck tones, at once amazed and terrfied, and no doubt feeling that, if indeed they *were* to be protected by the gods, they had nothing to lose by finally striking back at the hated whites.

Isatai bent and ran his questing fingers through the loose dirt midway between himself and Eagle Hand until he found what he was looking for – the still-warm .36-calibre bullet Eagle Hand had fired at him.

Lifting it high for all to see, he called, 'Now is the time to rise up and fight the whites until they are no more, my brothers! This is the will of the Sacred Powers – that we fight then, kill them, and then watch as Mother Earth opens her soil to swallow them whole! For only by destroying those who would destroy us will we ever truly know peace – a peace in which *P'te* will return in greater numbers than ever! This I say!'

The silence that followed his words lasted for little more than a second. Then Eagle Hand let go a piercing war cry, and this in turn became a signal to the rest of them. Warriors leapt to their feet, clenched their fists and yelled themselves hoarse, each man ready for war and anxious to kill as many whites as he could.

Caught up in the excitement of the moment, Quanah yelled louder than any of them.

Hennessy woke early the following morning, feeling stiff, achy and keen to move on. It had been a poor night at best, and he was glad when dawn finally threw its grey streamers across the eastern sky and he was able to get up, wash and leave the heady man-stink of the crowded barracks behind him.

He crossed to the mess hall, moving slowly because his battered muscles had seized up on him after all. This early the place was still empty, but Bill Olds and his wife were already busy preparing for the day ahead. As he ordered breakfast, Olds gave him a searching glance.

'They say you mixed it up with Hank Ketchum las' night,' he remarked. 'Lookin' at you this mornin', I can believe it.'

Hennessy shrugged. 'That was Ketchum's choice, not mine.'

'I can believe that, too. But if the talk's anythin' to

go by, it's not over yet, Mr Hennessy. Leastways, not as far as Hank's concerned. You figure to stay around here for any length o' time, you better learn to sleep with one eye open.'

'I'll remember that, but I'm not figuring to stay.'

'Then that's a lucky thing,' Olds allowed with feeling, 'for one of you.'

Hennessy ate in silence after that, chewing carefully in order to favour the cuts and swellings around his mouth and jaw. Twenty minutes later he bade the Oldses farewell and was closing the mess hall door behind him when he spotted a bearded man with greying hair whose name was Jim McInnery. He asked if McInnery had seen Billy Dixon anywhere.

'He lit out a little afore sunrise with them two fellers he's taken under his wing,' came the reply. Hennessy assumed he was referring to Bat Masterson and Oscar Sheppard. 'They was headed south, hopin' to pick up sign of anoth—'

McInnery stopped suddenly, having spotted Milt Hagerman leading his untidy chestnut horse from the communal corral. 'That *hombre* makes my skin crawl,' he confided in an undertone. 'Don't know the meanin' o' fear, jus' lives to kill.' Beneath his heavy moustache his lips formed into a sour line. 'You mark my words, Hennessy. Next time you see him, that bag he carries'll be full o' scalps again.'

'Someone should stop him,' Hennessy murmured.

'Before he kills some o' them new red friends o' yourn, you mean?' McInnery asked mockingly.

Refusing to be drawn, Hennessy pointed out, 'The

Comanches won't stand by and watch him slaughter their people forever. When they decide they've had enough, they'll make sure you all pay the price.'

'We'll be ready for 'em,' McInnery said confidently, and Hennessy had to smile mirthlessly when he heard that.

'Believe me, Jim,' he replied, 'mighty few men are *ever* ready when the Comanches come a-calling.'

As McInnery went on his way, Hennessy turned his attention back to Hagerman, who had just finished checking his rig one last time and was now dragging himself into the saddle, his sabre knocking gently against his long left leg. Cradling his Henry repeater across his lap and muttering all the while, he gave Hennessy a sharp nod and a phlegmy cackle as he walked the animal past.

Hennessy shook his head. It seemed that even Hagerman had made up his mind about him. But what the hell – let them think what they liked, be it Indian-lover or coward. He knew better, and that was the main thing. In any case, he figured he'd seen enough of Adobe Walls and its dollar-hungry residents for one visit, and that being the case, the only thing left for him to do was ride out after Billy and his two companions, say his goodbyes and then head for pastures new.

Billy, Bat Masterson and Oscar Sheppard drew rein at the foot of a rare, gentle rise, brought to a halt by a barely-audible rumble that seemed to rise and then fade on the early-morning breeze. Billy, watching as Masterson nudged his hat back and glanced skyward in

69

search of thunderheads, gave a low chuckle.

'Ain't no storm comin', boy,' he advised, putting his horse to the slope until he reached its brushy rim. 'Jus' get on up here, you two, an' point your eyes south a-ways.'

Billy dismounted, left his mount ground-hitched and sank to his haunches. When Masterson and Sheppard topped out behind him, he gestured that they should follow suit. 'That sound you can hear,' he said, 'that's *buffalo* comin', boys!'

Masterson quickly ran his pale blue eyes over the flats below. Beside him, Sheppard did likewise. Nothing moved on the vast, seemingly empty plain. Then Masterson saw something and opened his mouth to speak but quickly fell silent again. No, it was just a funnel of dust, stirred up by the warm breeze – what they called a *willy-way* in these parts.

A moment later, however, Oscar Sheppard stiffened. He'd seen the willy-way as well, but now he became aware of a dust cloud far behind it, hanging low to the ground but spreading higher, broader, even as he watched.

At the same moment he noticed something else, as well. The ominous rumbling sound was getting louder, and it was now interspersed with an occasional roar and bellow.

Billy watched as Masterson and Sheppard exchanged an expectant glance. They'd been at Adobe Walls long enough for him to get their measure, but were still very much newcomers to this game. As if to prove it, Masterson cried out when the ground beneath them started to vibrate, and again Billy laughed at him.

'That's jus' the king o' the prairie approachin', my friends,' he murmured. 'The king we intend to *depose*.'

Then even Billy, who had seen the sight more times than he could recall, fell into an spellbound silence as, from out of the dust cloud, came a long, lumbering line of huge, heavy-shouldered buffalo, shaggy-coated, hump- and slope-backed, with curved horns and tufted beards; a hundred of them, two hundred, maybe five hundred, flowing across the prairie in a steady mud-brown and cinnamon-coloured tide.

Sheppard murmured, 'My God. . . .'

Ahead and on the flanks of the herd came the bulls, with their huge, low-hanging heads, beady, fringe-covered eyes and black, curved horns. Tipping the scales at around a ton each, they were feisty now, for the mating season was close and the urge to multiply was strong in them. Some were using their horns to dig into the dirt and fling dust back over their massive backs to dislodge parasites. Others occasionally stopped to roll through the dust and short grass like horses, hoping to achieve much the same aim, and there wasn't one among them that didn't stand at least ten feet from tip to tail and six or more feet to the shoulder.

Younger spike bulls shuffled along in among the cows and reddish-brown calves, still minding their manners but already starting to show signs of self-assurance and the willingness to dominate those around them. The cows themselves, weighing in at around a thousand pounds, were somewhat smaller than the bulls, but still around eight feet long and the better part of five feet to the shoulder. Some calves, already a fair size, stuck close to their mothers. Others, now weaned, made their own way, some in groups of about twenty, others in smaller bunches.

As the first few buffalo began to pass the high ground upon which the three men were crouched, Sheppard said worriedly, 'Hadn't we better take cover, Billy? Don't want to spook 'em.'

Billy shook his head. 'The Good Lord gave the buffalo many things, Oscar, but He didn't give 'em much in the way of eyesight.' Warming to the subject, he continued, 'Why, I've snuck in close enough to reach out an' scratch one o' them prairie cows before now, an' they never even knowed I was there. Not that I'd advise such behaviour, o' course. When they spook, they spook good, an' a man wouldn't last long among 'em once they gets to runnin'.'

'You think they might smell us, though?' Sheppard pursued with concern.

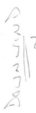

'We're upwind of 'em,' Masterson pointed out absently, clearly fascinated by the procession.

The horses were starting to shy and sidestep now, and their masters had to push erect and restrain them. 'They're headed north,' Billy muttered, following the buffalos' line of march. 'An' that's where we'll find 'em comes noon! They'll walk 'emselves ragged, then settle on a decent bed-ground, an' that's when we'll have 'em, fellers! Good huntin' an' rich pickin's!'

Masterson's transparent eyes, with their very large,

very dark pupils, were bright with excitement at the prospect. Though he couldn't speak for Sheppard, this was certainly the reason *he* had come to Adobe Walls – to make money, a lot of money, and to make it fast! Already his breathing had dropped to a shallow panting.

'We oughta go after 'em,' he said, speaking half to himself. 'First ones to the herd'll make the money.'

'They's plenty enough to go around,' Billy replied. He ran an experienced eye over the animals. 'An' I 'spect it'll take us a week or more to whittle down a herd o' that size.'

At last the herd passed them by. The rumble began to fade again, the dust to settle, the ground to cease its vibrations. Still transfixed, Masterson tried to decide how many buffalo he'd seen. Six, seven hundred? More?

At last, reluctantly following Billy's example, he and Sheppard mounted up and turned their horses north. Masterson felt almost giddy with excitement, for the week ahead promised to bring not only valuable experience but also, if he was lucky, considerable wealth.

It was just like Billy had said – good hunting and rich pickings.

As Adobe Walls fell behind him, Hennessy called Billy Dixon seven kinds of fool for riding south into Comanche country at this of all times. Then again, he wasn't exactly showing much sense himself, chasing right after him in his present, beat-up condition. Still, he couldn't leave without saying goodbye. He and Billy might have their differences, but they'd travelled too many trails together for that.

The early morning chill hadn't taken long to evaporate, and the temperature now stood at a hundred energy-sapping degrees. Around him, the Staked Plains were slow-cooking beneath a merciless sun, and there was no movement other than that of Hennessy and his horse. That wasn't to say he had these vast high plains to himself, though. The Indians were out there somewhere, he felt sure: the best he could hope for right now was that he and they wouldn't cross trails.

Fortunately, Billy's tracks weren't hard to spot, and he soon had the gelding following them in a long, mile-eating trot. The air was like hot glue, the *Llano Estacado* itself filled with an almost overwhelming silence that was broken only by the regular, hollow clatter of the gelding's hoofs.

Around the middle of the morning Hennessy stopped to water the horse in the shade of a few stunted paloverde trees. He poured water into his up-turned hat, allowed the gelding to drink his fill and was just tying the canteen back around his saddle horn when he threw a casual glance north-east and saw them.

Indians.

They were still the better part of a mile away and, near as he could tell, there was a whole bunch of 'em. Worse still, it appeared to Hennessy as if they were headed straight for him.

He reacted instinctively, dragging the horse deeper into cover and hauling his Big Fifty from its scabbard. The Indians, meanwhile, seemed to hover on the far horizon, their shapes distorted by the dancing heat-waves.

Propping the heavy buffalo gun against the nearest tree, Hennessy pulled a sack of greased cartridges from his near-side saddlebag and dropped it at his feet. If all he'd heard was true, the Fifty had a way of spooking the Indians, who had heard stories about its power, range and accuracy and learned to treat it with respect.

Next he grabbed the gelding's nose and dosed his palm around its big, flared nostrils, for even the slight-est sound could alert the Indians to his presence – assuming they hadn't already spotted him, of course.

In next to no time the Indians had come within a couple-hundred yards of the paloverdes, and were still holding their horses to a steady, determined lope. Any moment now he expected them to fan out and rush him. Hearing the approaching hoof beats and wanting to show himself and make friends, the gelding strug-gled a little, but Hennessy tightened his grip and in a sharp whisper told the animal to hold still.

The Indians came on, still bunched together. With his free hand, Hennessy reached down to release the thong on the Colt's hammer.

And then, just when he least expected it, they veered eastward.

He knew a brief, heady moment of relief then, when it became clear that they hadn't seen him after all, and obviously had business elsewhere. As they cantered past, however, now no more than a hundred yards from where he stood frozen, he got his first good look at their deerskin hip leggings and finely-crafted moccasins, their cotton shirts and beaded belts, from which hung buffalo tails and white feathers, and his uneasiness suddenly returned with a vengeance.

He'd been expecting Comanches, or maybe Kiowa, but these were neither. Their height and dress suggested another tribe – Arapaho. And by the way they were pushing their ponies through this punishing heat, they were in a hurry to get where they were going.

It was their hurry, he thought, that had probably kept them from spotting him.

Only when they'd gone did he release his breath and deflate a fraction. But the Indians had left him with a number of questions. What had brought them here, into Comanche and Kiowa territory? The Arapahos were nomads, it was true, and they'd been known to trade with the Comanches in the past. But they were also known for their hostility towards both the Comanches and Kiowas. And now that he thought about it, they'd certainly had the look of a raiding party.

Were they here to make war, then?

He really didn't know. It could as easily be that they were just passing through. But if so, where were they headed, and what mischief did they have planned for when they got there?

He sleeved his sweat-run face. Whatever they were up to, he felt the men of Adobe Walls should be told about it, just in case it was linked to the Indian trouble he'd run into yesterday.

He thought for a moment about whether he should turn back or go on, made his decision and swung back into the saddle. Checking to make sure the Arapaho were no longer in sight, he broke cover and continued following Billy's tracks.

FIVE

It was Billy who saw him first, but it was Masterson who tried to shoot him.

Still busy thinking about all the money he stood to make over the next week or so, Masterson went for his gun as soon as they emerged from between two sand hills and spotted him. It was only the harsh bark of Billy's voice that froze him before the gun could clear leather.

'No call to burn powder, boy! That's Hennessy!'

Startled, Masterson reined in fast, took another squint at the distant horseman and saw his mistake.

But as he allowed the weapon to drop back into leather, the Illinois-born youngster curled his lip. He didn't fully understand it himself, but there was something about Hennessy he just couldn't warm to. Maybe it was because he sensed that the feeling was mutual. Or maybe he just hated the idea that Hennessy had been so quick to dismiss him as a know-nothing greenhorn.

Grudgingly, he said, 'Sorry, Billy. I thought he was a Comanche.'

Billy had shortened his own rein by now. 'Well, next time, you jus' remember to make damn' sure of your man before you decide to put him down.'

The reprimand hit him like a slap. 'I said I was sorry,' he bristled.

A few moments later, Hennessy brought his mount to a sliding halt before them, nodded a terse greeting and then told Billy what he'd seen. Billy listened grimly, knowing better than to ask if Hennessy was sure about it. Hennessy wouldn't make a mistake about something like that, any more'n he would.

'How many were there?' he asked when Hennessy fell silent.

'About two dozen'd be my guess. Carrying rifles too, most of 'em.'

Billy smacked one palm down on his saddle horn. 'They would have to show up now, wouldn't they?' he growled. 'Just when we've hit paydirt!'

'I'd worry more about keeping my hair, was I you,' Hennessy advised mildly. 'Best we get on back to Adobe Walls and spread the word.'

'Where's the hurry?' asked Masterson, as Hennessy made to turn his horse around. 'What's to say them red bastards ain't just passin' through, headed for Mexico?'

Hennessy gave him another of those looks he was learning to hate, the kind of look that said he wasn't just dumb, he was downright stupid. 'Because this is the time of the Sun Dance, boy,' Hennessy explained.

Oscar Sheppard frowned. 'An' you think the Arapaho plan to take part?' he hazarded, breaking his usual shy silence.

'I think they might be hopin' to forge some kind of alliance with the Comanches and the Kiowas while they're all gathered together for the ceremony,' Hennessy replied. 'Join forces so's they can wipe you folks off the map.'

Billy chewed on that for a spell. 'That'd sure make sense,' he allowed after a moment. Then: 'You're right, Cal. We better warn the others. Then we'll fort up for a couple days, see what happens next.'

'What about the herd?' demanded Masterson. 'We jus' gonna let it go?'

'Them buffalo won't stray far,' predicted Billy. 'Any case, we got first claim.'

Masterson snorted at that. He knew that most hide runners of any experience worked to a simple, unwritten agreement: that you never muscled in on another hunter's stand, especially if he'd staked his claim first. You respected that claim just as you expected him to respect yours.

But if Masterson knew anything about men, it was that they were always ready to earn an extra dollar, and the rules be damned. Hell, if the position was reversed and the reward great enough, he wasn't even sure he could trust himself to do the right thing.

But there was no time to argue the point now. The others, apparently not sharing his misgivings, had already pointed their horses for home, and he had to move fast to catch up with them.

'Tell us, Quanah,' said Lone Wolf. 'When do you intend to attack the white man's fort?'

Satanta nodded, eager for the answer. 'You know that we of the Kiowa will follow you!'

Quanah hesitated before replying. Isatai had given them a sign. More importantly, he had given them proof of his claims. And yet, as caught up in the lust for war as he had been the night before, he was still reluctant to commit his people to battle.

Sensing as much for himself, Satanta noted perceptively, 'You think of the weak. Of those who will mourn their dead. And this does you credit, Quanah. But you must understand just how much worse things will become for the *Nermernuh*, if you do *not* act now!

'Remember what happened to my own people,' he continued, his voice suddenly thickening. 'They forced us to dwell upon a reservation we had no desire to inhabit and made us grow "Indian corn" to survive! But was that any way for our people to live, Quanah? Of course not! We are not farmers, we are warriors! We must fight, for if we do not, we are nothing!'

Quanah was just about to reply, to suggest perhaps a few exploratory skirmishes here and there to gauge the strength of the enemy and their willingness to fight, when he became aware of an excited babble outside. Rising gracefully, he pushed out of the *tipi* and into the hard daylight, with Lone Wolf and Satanta at his heels.

His warriors were grabbing for their weapons, anxious to arm themselves quickly. Spotting him, one hurried over and pointed to the jagged canyon rim where Eagle Hand stood watch. 'Arapaho are coming. Quanah!' he reported. 'Perhaps five hands of them – and they wear the colours of war!'

81

Dismissing the man with a nod, Quanah broke away from his companions and followed a barely discernible path up towards the canyon-rim in a series of fluid, loping strides. He knew the Arapaho as men of honour, but the news of their warpaint concerned him. Arapaho and Comanche had fought before, many times. But oftener still they had traded together and come to share an unspoken bond of trust and respect.

He could think of no reason why they might wish to make war at this time. They were perhaps the most religious of all the tribes, and of all the ceremonies they observed, none was more important to them than the Sun Dance. It did not seem likely to him that they would soil such a sacred time with bloodshed.

Was it possible, then, that they had come because they wished to take part in the rites and rituals being held here? But if so, why were they painted for war?

He reached the spot from which Eagle Hand had sounded the alarm. Eagle Hand watched him climb, then indicated the position of the newcomers with one long finger when he finally came to a halt. At the approximate centre of the exposed flats below, a group of riders, barely visible in the gauzy loud of dust raised by their horses' hoofs, were heading directly towards the canyon entrance. There were, as he had been told, in excess of twenty warriors.

Quanah felt Eagle Hand's eyes upon him. Eagle Hand, he thought, who had taken it upon himself to kill two whites the day before and returned to the camp as a hero because of it. Eagle Hand, who had been chosen to help Isatai prove the gods' promise of invulnerability. Eagle Hand, who might very well become the next leader of the Kwahadis, if he didn't make the decision – the right decision – soon.

The newcomers were now close enough for him to see them more clearly. At their head rode a tall, slim Arapaho whose face was daubed with red paint. Recognizing him, Quanah quickly picked a path down off the rim and onto the brushy flats that led towards the canyon, intending to intercept them.

Inasmuch as a Comanche could ever give his friendship to someone other than a fellow Comanche, he and this man could be called friends, and that was some comfort to him. Coming down onto the canyon floor, he planted himself in the riders' path and waited until they drew rein before him. But when they did so, he saw an eagerness in the Arapahos that was coupled with a barely-suppressed anger that made for a dangerous mixture, and all at once he was on his guard again.

'I welcome you, Wo'teen,' he said carefully, addressing the leader of the group. The Arapaho were a polite people, and it was as well to observe the formalities with them. 'My heart is glad to see you here. But when I look at your face, I see no joy. Your eyes flash with hatred.'

Wo'teen slid from his pony's back and raised his right hand, signifying that he came in peace, despite the paint worn by him and his men. He was in his early thirties, tall and handsome but for an overlarge aquiline nose. He wore red circles on his forehead and cheeks, and the centre parting of his jet-black hair, which was worn in two braids, typical Arapaho style, was also coloured red.

'It is good to see you again, my brother,' he replied. 'But you are right. I come to this place with war in my heart.'

'What has happened?' asked Quanah.

'A few days ago, a band of white men attacked our camp, killed three of our people and stole twenty and more of our horses, fine buckskins all. We have been tracking them ever since, and believe now that the trail leads towards the fort the whites call Adobe Walls.'

'These thieves were buffalo hunters, then?'

'This I do not know. We lost their trail in a dust storm. But what else can I believe? In any case, even if we are wrong there can be no denying that these hunters have stolen from us in other ways.'

Quanah nodded. 'The land,' he agreed. 'The buffalo.'

'Whether they killed our people and stole our horses or not,' Wo'teen continued, 'we are angry, and feel that we have taken *enough* from them.' His eyes turned bleak as he concluded, 'We – that is, those of us you see before you now – have decided to kill them all before they can steal any more. But we are small in number, Quanah. If you would join us, our victory would be the greater, and more certain.'

Quanah frowned. Was this another sign, he wondered, another way in which the gods were seeking to tell him the course he should take? Not knowing made him feel frustrated and helpless.

One way or another, however, the decision had to be

made, and if he failed to make it or kept postponing the moment, he would lose face.

Glancing back at the canyon rim and seeing Eagle Hand staring down at him, he realized he might lose even more.

He looked behind him. His people and their guests had crowded into the canyon entrance to discover for themselves the reason for the Arapahos' visit. He saw Satanta among them, and Lone Wolf. He saw the impassive Cheyenne chieftain Stone Calf and a scattering of other Comanche leaders, such as Grey Beard and Big Bow, White Shield, Mow-way, Tai-hai-ya-Tai, Wild Horse, Isahabeet and Howling Wolf.

And there, hanging back in the crowd, he saw also the long, skeletal face of Isatai, watching him curiously.

'The crime against you is a crime against us, also,' he said finally, turning his attention back to the Arapahos and weighing his words with care. 'Our hearts, like yours, also cry out for justice – and so it is war, my brother!

'Piece by piece we will destroy the whites together! Together we will destroy them all!'

Hennessy soon had Masterson pegged for a fool. In this country, where horseflesh was worth more than its weight in gold and a man afoot was a dead man who just didn't know it yet, only a fool pushed his horse as hard as Masterson was pushing his right now. Billy noticed it too, and after a while called Masterson's name.

Without slowing, the youngster hipped around. 'What?'

'This ain't a race, boy. Go easy on your mount.'

Masterson faced front again, muttering darkly under his breath, but from that moment on he held his mount to the long, pacing stride of his three companions, and sometime around mid-afternoon Adobe Walls at last appeared on the horizon.

A few moments later they passed through the crumbling walls, and Billy dragged his Remington New Model Army .44 from his belt and sent a shot skyward to sound the alarm.

That brought hide men running from all points, and started the Newfoundland dog barking and turning excited circles over by the wagon owned by his masters, a pair of brothers named Isaac and Jacob Scheidler. After a while, Mike Welch pushed through the chattering crowd and grabbed the cheek-strap of Billy's horse to hold the skittish animal steady, and all at once the babble faded to silence.

'What is it, Billy?' Mike asked in his slow, deep rumble. 'More trouble?'

'Could be,' said Billy.

He told them all what Hennessy had seen, and what it most likely signified, and as they digested that, he added, 'If you boys'll take my advice, you'll fort up here till we know how this thing's gonna play out.' He frowned suddenly, sat a little straighter and ran his dark eyes across his audience. 'Who's missin', anyway?'

A man called California Joe Milner said, 'Johnny Bourke and his crew lit out earlier this mornin'. Johnny said he wanted to get his skins to Dodge before the price dropped.'

Billy tucked his tongue into his cheek while he thought about that. 'Well,' he decided after a moment, 'they should be safe enough, I reckon. That's a seven-man crew Johnny's got, an' they's none of 'em a slouch with a rifle. Anyone else?'

Someone offered Milt Hagerman's name, and Mike Welch added, 'Hank Ketchum's party, too.'

'Ketchum? Where the hell did *he* go?'

'Reckons he found hisseif a middlin' herd about fifteen miles south-east. Figured to get out there today, see if he could make a decent stand of it.'

'When did they leave?' demanded Billy.

'First light, thereabouts.'

'You reckon they'll be awright, Mr Dixon?' called Mrs Olds, who was standing beside her husband on the far fringe of the crowd, twisting worriedly at the material of her apron.

'The only thing I'd say for sure,' replied Billy, 'is that we can't afford to lose three more men. If this thing comes to a fight, we're gonna need every gun we can get. Which means,' and here his voice dropped a notch, because he didn't like having to say it any more than the men around him were going to like hearing it, 'someone better go fetch 'em in while they' still there for the fetchin'.'

The assembled men glanced uneasily at each other, and Hennessy saw that they were at last starting to realize that what had happened to Dudley and Williams the day before hadn't just been an isolated incident after all: that the arrival of even more Indians in these parts today had suddenly made the possibility of an

Indian attack seem altogether more likely. That being the case, few of them wanted to leave the relative safety of Adobe Walls right now, especially for the likes of Hank Ketchum and his crew.

Hennessy couldn't blame them. These men weren't fighters by profession.

They only shot at critters who couldn't shoot back. But Billy had a point. Three more guns could make all the difference if it came to kill-or-be-killed.

As the heavy silence stretched into half a minute, he blew air through his nose. 'All right,' he said, telling himself he really ought to know better. 'I'll chance it. Anyone game enough to go with me?'

'I'll go,' said Masterson.

Hennessy shook his head. 'Thanks, but no thanks.'

Masterson went stiff. 'The hell you say!'

'You'll stay put, Bat,' snapped Billy.

'I'll do it if you'll give me one good reason why!'

' 'Cause right now you're about as green as unsunned pumpkins, boy, an' that's the truth of it,' Billy told him evenly. 'If Hennessy does this, he'll need men to back him, not a kid to nursemaid.'

That was too much for Masterson. For a moment his eyes went wide and he looked as if he might throw himself at Billy. Instead he yanked his reins around and spurred his horse through the crowd and over towards Hanrahan's saloon, where he dismounted and stamped angrily inside.

When he was gone, Bermuda Carlisle shouldered forward and said, 'You can count me in, Hennessy.'

'Me too,' said a bull-necked *hombre* Hennessy knew

as Harvey O'Neal.

Hennessy nodded tiredly. 'Obliged,' he said, and meant it.

It took only minutes for him to switch horses, and for his companions to grab their guns and cut out a pair of strong mounts for themselves. When they set out again, following the tracks left by Ketchum and his wagon, Hennessy allowed himself a fleeting smile and a weary shake of the head. Funny how things worked out sometimes, he thought. Yesterday he'd whupped Ketchum good, before Ketchum could whup *him*. Now, as hot and pained and tired of violence as he was, he was risking his life to save that of the self-same man.

Could be that Masterson wasn't the only fool in these parts.

There was one brief moment on the journey out from Adobe Walls when Hank Ketchum thought he'd made a mistake in coming out at all. The day was shaping up to be hotter than Hell's hinges, and the beating he'd received the previous evening had taken more out of him than he'd realized.

But the feeling didn't last long. Money was money, after all, and for the tall, white-haired Ketchum, that's what this business was all about. A natural competitor, it was one of the reasons he liked to get first claim as often as he could: so's he could kill more buffalo and make more money than the other feller.

For as long as he cared to remember, it had always been his practice to scout around for handy little bonus herds, and he'd been scouting for one – without noticeable success – ever since he'd brought his crew out to Adobe Walls a few weeks earlier. But the previous day he'd finally chanced upon a seep that dribbled between layers of exposed rock to feed a thin stream, and something had told him his luck was about to change.

Poor as it was, the water supply had led him on to a well-worn buffalo trail, the trail on to an area which had been substantially grazed, and about an hour after that he had finally come upon his elusive bonus herd itself.

The buffalo were stretched out across a shallow bowl of grassland fringed by scrub and stunted cottonwoods, rolling or flicking their tails to dislodge pests, or simply chewing the cud, and a rough tally had told him that there were between eighty and a hundred of them.

So he'd returned to Adobe Walls in good humour and told his two skinners, gaunt-faced Daniel Garland and Avery Hicks, a beanpole of a fellow with pale skin and a constantly bobbing Adam's apple, to have the wagon loaded and ready to move by sun-up, 'cause they'd be pulling out just after first light next day.

Of course, he hadn't figured on getting the worst of his run-in with Hennessy first. Rolling out of his blankets this morning, he'd found himself stiff as a board and hardly able to move for the pain it caused him. But there'd be time to settle things with that bastard once the bonus herd was taken care of, and that prospect, even more than the money he stood to make, made his assorted hurts a mite easier to carry.

Ketchum's modest crew and his seen-better-days

light wagon, loaded down with all the tools of their trade, including spare ammunition, extra guns, skinning blades, chains, sledgehammers and grindstones, had quit Adobe Walls a little after sunrise, and Ketchum, riding ahead astride a mercifully docile buckskin horse, had led the way out to the bonus herd.

Now he was ready to spend the morning killing as many buffalo as he could.

With the wagon parked well back from the herd, Garland and Hicks got a fire going and started boiling coffee. There'd be no skinning work till the killing work was done, so all they could do was wait. Moving carefully in order to favour his bruises, Ketchum himself collected his gear, a long Sharps .50/.90, the iron fork upon which he would rest and steady the weight of the heavy weapon, and a bag of greased metallic cartridges, which would not only put a buffalo down if you hit him just right, but would *keep* him down, too.

'Well,' he said at length. 'Let's go get rich.'

And as he nodded, 'So long', he saw his own rising blood-lust reflected in the faces of his skinners.

He found good cover in a run of saltbush, from which he had an unobstructed view across the bowl of land in which the herd had settled. The buffalo were completely unaware of his presence. As he studied them through his cool green eyes, all Ketchum felt – aside from the heavy excitement that always came before the slaughter, of course – was an overwhelming sense of contempt. *Look at them,* he thought. Ignorant of what was about to happen, and so stupid that the survivors wouldn't even learn from it. Big, shaggy bastards, they deserved all they got.

He went down on his belly, a big man with long, heavy arms and legs, shoved the iron fork into the ground before him and settled the Sharps's long, octagonal barrel into its supportive V, then took a while observing the conditions, mentally calculating angles to compensate for windage and elevation. When he was satisfied, he reached into the bag and brought out a single centre-fire cartridge that was almost three inches long. He loaded it into the Sharps, then, scratching thoughtfully at his curly, iron-grey beard, he studied the herd some more.

Bulls, dams, calves – it made no never-mind to Ketchum. He'd make money from all of them. But what he was looking for now was the nearest thing the big shaggies had to a leader, the one who was just canny enough to sound the alarm before Ketchum had killed enough of them.

He settled eventually on a big old bull grazing on the far edge of the herd, who constantly raised his massive head so that he could keep a watchful eye on their surroundings. He was the one. And that meant he must be the first to die.

Ketchum sighted along the weapon, searching for the right spot for his bullet, the spot that would put the bull down swiftly and without fuss. He waited until the animal was broadside on to him, chose a point just beyond which the animal's ribcage ended and then gently squeezed the trigger. The Sharps gave a roar and punched back into his right shoulder. He took it with a curse, watched just long enough to see the bull collapse in a heap, shot through the lungs and already bleeding from the nose, then calmly reloaded.

Incredibly, the animals milling around the old bull paid him no mind, and showed no signs of panic. One of them poked curiously at the dying beast with its moist snout, then simply moved on. Having had little if any previous contact with man, they simply didn't have the first clue as to what had just happened – or what was still to happen.

Over the next hour or so, the morning peace was shattered time and again by the steady, rhythmic tattoo of the big man's rifle: huge, rolling reports that carried for a mile or more on the hot, still air, and after each crash a buffalo dropped, quivering, to the valley floor, fatally wounded or killed outright.

A calf about the size of a large dog finally sensed that something wasn't quite right and started searching for its mother. But the dam, so alive just moments before, now lay motionless on the ground, bleeding from a large, ragged wound in her side that was already filling with hungry flies.

A second later Ketchum claimed the calf as well, the force of the bullet slamming right through the creature and flinging it to one side.

Gunpowder and blood began to foul the air as the slaughter went on and the buffalo continued to fall. Load, aim, fire, reload. . . . On and on it went, until at last Ketchum's trigger-finger started to blister and his rifle barrel grew so hot that he had to climb stiffly to his knees and urinate on it to cool it down again.

In almost no time, the better part of fifty buffalo lay dead or dying, but the rest of the herd was finally starting to turn restless and fidgety. Any minute now they'd start moving, ponderously at first but then with greater urgency, as some vague, half-understood sense of alarm at last communicated itself to them.

Ketchum shot another three buffalo, and then the rest began to mill around and gradually break into an aimless, shuffling run.

Slick with sweat, he ran a sleeve across his whiskery mouth and watched them go. They'd run for a time, but they'd not go far. When he and the boys were finished here, they'd catch the herd again and then he'd see the job through to the end.

He shoved himself erect, grunting with effort, and bawled, 'All right, fellers – time to earn your pay!'

And while he stretched and walked around awhile to ease the knots in his muscles, Garland and Hicks set to work, bringing up the wagon and then picking their way from body to body, making sure the buffalo each man was about to skin really *was* dead, and not just wounded or still in the process of dying.

One or the other of them would make a close inspection of the beast and, if in doubt, would use a knife to finish it off. Then he'd make his first cut from the lower jaw, down the neck and straight along the belly until he reached a spot just below the tail. He'd score the inside of each leg then, and finally begin the business of peeling the hide back with a knife specially curved for the purpose.

Both men worked swiftly and without error. They'd

done this so many times, they could have probably done it blindfolded. At last, with the carcass rolled over and the hide all but removed, all that remained was to tie a line around the skin still attached to the buffalo's hump and then use one of the team-horses to tear it free.

The hide was rolled then, and thrown into the back of the wagon. Later, when they got back to Adobe Walls, it would be stretched or pegged out, meat-side down, to dry. While he was about it, Garland also cut several heavy slabs of tender hump-meat for Mrs Olds.

Ketchum helped himself to a mug of stewed black coffee and blew steam off its surface. The bowl of land before him was littered with bodies, most of them pink and hairless now, glistening red in the hard sunlight and crawling with flies.

At length he set his mug down, spat into his palms and rubbed them together. He'd go give the boys a hand, just to speed things up, and then get back to the killing.

But just then his buckskin stopped grazing, looked up and shook his big head. Ketchum frowned at the animal, wondering what he'd seen or smelled to make him fret. He threw a brief glance southward, the direction which seemed to have claimed the horse's interest, and was just about to turn his attention back to the horse when he suddenly froze.

Holy mother of Christ.

Sky-lined on a ridge about half a mile away sat twenty mounted Indians armed with lances, bows, hatchets, handguns and rifles.

SIX

They sat absolutely still, just watching, and allowing the vague breeze to stir their feathers and ruffle their horses' manes, and Ketchum, suddenly unable to tear his eyes away from them, felt something heavy and nauseating settle in his stomach. How long had they been there? And what did they have in mind for when they were all through watching?

Carefully, he reached into his bag, brought out a greased cartridge and fumbled it into the Sharps, all the time edging towards the valley rim. 'Garland!' he called in a weird sort of half-shout, half-whisper.

Garland, about fifty yards away, was too engrossed in his work to hear him.

'*Garland!*'

At last the skinner straightened up and turned at the waist, a tall, lean man with sunken cheeks and a large nose. 'What's that you say?' he called.

Ketchum was about to reply when the Indians suddenly split into two groups, one headed west, the other east, and all at once he knew *exactly* what they had in mind. They were going to hit them on the flanks and make them divide their firepower between the two bands.

'*Indians!*' he yelled, and threw himself down the gentle slope in a clumsy run towards the cover of the wagon, the weight of the Sharps dragging at his arms.

A split second later both Garland and Hicks saw them too, and throwing down their knives, they also sprinted for the wagon. They were about halfway there when the first lot of Indians charged over the rim and down into the bowl itself, bunched up at first but then fanning out and screeching at the tops of their lungs as they sent their horses leaping over the dead buffaloes in their path.

Knowing he was never going to make it in time, Hicks turned, clawed a .36-calibre Navy Starr out of his belt and fired at the leading Indian. He didn't hit the man but he hit the horse, and it went down, forelegs first, and did an ungainly kind of head-over-heels that threw its rider sideways out of his buffalo-pelt saddle. The Indian hit the ground hard and rolled a couple of times, then came back up, dazed but still screaming, and Hicks fired again, and managed to hit him smack in the face.

The Indian's head exploded in a red mist and he fell backwards. Hicks yelled a triumphant, '*Yes!*', but in the next moment another Indian was bearing down on him, coming in at a gallop, and his red-painted face was twisted into a mask of raw hatred.

The Indian skewered Hicks through the belly with a feather-decorated lance, and Hicks yelled like a banshee and crashed to the ground, heels drumming as his hands groped uselessly at the shaft of the lance. Something pink and wet started oozing from the wound, and a thick trail of blood trickled from his grotesquely-contorted mouth. He was dead within perhaps half a minute.

But by then Garland had made it to the wagon, thrown himself underneath it and was dragging an octagonal-barrelled Tranter from his belt, determined to give Ketchum some covering fire on his way in.

One of the charging braves had other ideas, though. Drawing rein, he brought up a heavy Walker Colt, drew a bead on Ketchum and fired, but missed. Ketchum didn't wait for him to try his luck again, he just kept running for the wagon, moving faster than he'd ever thought possible. When he got there he threw himself flat, scurried under the vehicle beside Garland and then jammed the butt of the Sharps to his shoulder.

He snap-aimed at the Indian, whose excited horse was now turning in a tight circle. A second later the long gun boomed and the bullet smashed through the brave's right leg, spiralled on through his horse and, as it exited on the far side, blew his left foot off at the ankle. The horse died instantly and dropped as if boneless. The Indian screamed and writhed beside it.

He'd take a little longer to die.

The remaining Indians were circling the wagon now, screaming fit to bust their eardrums and making the ground shake beneath them. Desperately Garland thrust his gun to arm's length and fired. More by accident than design, a young Comanche was torn from horseback as though struck by a gigantic, invisible fist.

But two more Arapahos were already leaping from their horses and charging at them a-foot with weapons held high. With no time to reload the Sharps, Ketchum grabbed his holstered Smith and Wesson and fired twice.

He killed the first of the oncoming Indians right on the spot, but missed the second as the brave threw himself to his knees and loosed off an arrow. The shaft whistled through the air with a high, sharp, slicing sound and tore across Ketchum's right shoulder, ripping buckskin and flesh but doing no irreparable damage.

Ketchum, firing reflexively, tore the top of the bowman's skull off and sent him toppling. With a sudden rush of optimism he yelled. 'We can *do* this. Dan! We can *beat* these bastards!'

In the very next second, however, Garland gave a scream and flipped over, hit in the right arm by a flung tomahawk. The blade had bitten deep, though not quite deep enough to sever the limb. Still, the pain of it was overpowering, blanketing every other sense, and it sent Garland scrambling out from beneath the wagon, hugging his loose arm tight to his side and screaming for someone please for the love of God to help him.

'Dan! Get back under here!'

Garland didn't hear him. Disorientated by shock, he was no longer able to think straight, and just stumbled a few more paces, still screaming for someone to help him. As he moved, the tomahawk in his arm wobbled a bit and then fell from the wound to land at his dragging feet.

99

He was still screaming when one of the mounted Comanches rode him down.

He collided hard with the galloping horse and slammed backwards under the impact, and the horse's heavy, unshod hooves kicked him into a limp back-roll that just about finished the job. Then the Indian was gone and Garland was more of a broken doll than anything else, and the only thing Ketchum could think was, *Oh my Christ they're gone, they're both gone, I'm all alone—*

An instant later there was a thud that was all but drowned by the noise around him, and the wagon above him gave a shudder. One of the Indians had leapt into the wagon itself to see what treasures it contained, and that was almost more than he could bear. With a roar he rolled onto his back, pointed the Smith and Wesson at the boards and fired twice through the woodwork. He heard a scream, another thud, and felt a savage kind of joy to know that he'd greased another of the bastards.

Before he could savour the moment, however, rough hands damped around his ankles and hauled him out of cover and into the hammering afternoon sunlight. He wriggled like an eel, but they had him now and they had him *good.* A moment later he found himself staring up into three painted faces, felt the searing hatred from six hostile eyes and he screamed, because he knew now that this was how it was going to end for him: that there were going to be no more years or months, no more days, hours or minutes.

He had just seconds left to live.

*

At Hennessy's sudden signal, his companions drew rein behind him. A moment later they heard it, too – a faraway mixture of war-cry and gunfire.

'Sounds like we're too late,' muttered Carlisle, spitting to one side.

Hennessy raised an eyebrow. 'You want to turn back?'

Carlisle caught the challenge in the question and resolutely shook his head. He was a little cannon-ball of a man about forty years old, squat and big-bellied, with short arms and long dark hair, and though there was fear in his grey eyes, there was determination, too. 'Hell with that.' he said stiffly.

'Then let's ride.'

Hesitating for just a moment longer, Carlisle and O'Neal exchanged a tight glance. They were still half-convinced that Hennessy was in league with the Indians, and weren't sure just how far they could trust him. But then, following Hennessy's lead, they kicked their horses back to speed, leaving a great yellow streamer of dust in their wake as they crossed the flats at a ground-eating lope.

After a while the land rose towards a gentle hill. From here the war cries sounded louder, but the gunfire seemed to have petered out entirely. Halfway to the top Hennessy pulled up, dismounted and passed his reins to O'Neal. 'You wait here,' he murmured, dragging his Winchester from its sheath. 'I'll take a look-see over yonder rise.'

Carlisle, not much liking the idea of letting Hennessy go off on his own, also cooled his saddle.

'Reckon I'll go with you,' he said in a low voice.

Hennessy shrugged. 'Your choice. Just be ready to move fast if you have to.'

He waited for Carlisle to unlimber his big buffalo gun, then headed for the rim above in a fast crouch-run.

They were almost there when the war cries died away completely and all at once there was nothing save near-absolute quiet. Hennessy immediately went down behind some scrub. Carlisle quickly joined him. The buffalo hunter's eyes asked a question, but not having any sure answer for him, Hennessy could only shrug. A long half-minute passed, and still all was silent but for the buzz of yellow-jackets and the whine of cicadas in the sun-browned grass.

Then, without warning, there came a long, drawn-out scream that sent a winter's chill through both men, and suddenly it seemed to Hennessy that his skin was too small to accommodate his body.

'Like I said,' Carlisle muttered hoarsely, clenching one fist. 'We're too late.'

Hennessy peered through the brush. There was no one around that he could see and no one that he could sense, so he broke cover and continued up towards the far rim. Carlisle hesitated a moment, then went after him. Just before he topped out, Hennessy went down and snaked the rest of the way on his stomach. Once again Carlisle followed suit, breathing heavily now.

They stopped on the far side of some full-grown brittlebush and looked down through its confusion of yellow flowers into the bowl of land beyond. The ground was littered with the bodies of fifty or more buffalo, nearly all of them stripped to the red meat and left to rot. In among the carcasses was a scattering of human dead, too, both white man and red: even a horse.

Other men were still very much alive down there, though – a knot of about sixteen Indians, some still mounted, some afoot, two of them nursing what appeared to be gunshot wounds. And they were all gathered around the single survivor of their attack, a white man who lay some yards from an old covered wagon.

Hank Ketchum.

'Aw, Christ . . .' muttered Carlisle. 'Them red sons-abitches. . . .'

Hennessy was inclined to agree. The Indians had stripped Ketchum naked and then pegged him out on the hard, hot earth, so that his arms and legs were stretched wide. He was screaming while they worked on him, and it made Hennessy's teeth ache to hear such a Godawful mixture of howl and sob, plea and shriek.

The Indians didn't have any objections, though. To them it was the perfect accompaniment to the agonies they were inflicting upon their captive – the slicing off of a finger here, a toe there, an ear, a lip, his nose.

Carlisle suddenly clapped a hand over his mouth. Hennessy glanced at him. said, 'You all right?'

Above the line of his hand, Carlisle's eyes looked haunted, his skin pale and sweaty. Not trusting himself

103

to speak, he just gave a single, sick-looking nod.

Hennessy turned his attention back to the Indians and their red plaything below. Sixteen of the bastards, he thought. Too many to take on and hope to beat, even with the element of surprise on their side.

Quickly he considered their options. They didn't have all that many, so it didn't take very long. And when he finally reached his inevitable decision, he felt pretty much like puking himself.

'Go back to the horses,' he whispered. 'Tie mine tight to some brush and then you and O'Neal get the hell out of here.'

Carlisle swallowed hard. 'What about you?' he asked suspiciously. 'They's nothin' we can do here. The Indians've already killed Garland an' Hicks, an' Hank's as good as dead himself.'

But Carlisle couldn't have been more wrong. 'Hank's probably more alive now than he's ever been, though it's for sure he wishes he wasn't.' Hennessy told him through set teeth. 'And the Indians'll keep him that way for as long as it pleasures 'em.'

Carlisle's eyebrows met in a frown. 'Then what—?'

He was going to ask what Hennessy thought he could do about it, but in the same moment he realized exactly what he could do.

'Oh Lord,' he breathed. 'You're gonna kill him, ain't you?'

'I'm going to put him out of his misery,' Hennessy corrected him as, down below. Hank screamed again. 'Lessen you'd prefer to do it?'

Carlisle looked as if he'd been scalded. 'I got even

less stomach for it than you have. But if you shoot *him*, you'll bring the Indians down on *us*.'

'That's why I want you two to get out of here *now*. Head back for Adobe Walls and tell 'em what happened here, and to expect the worst. I'll be right behind you – I hope.'

Carlisle ran his callused palm down his sweaty face again. 'It's gonna be hell,' he whispered. 'Pullin' the trigger, I mean.'

Hennessy nodded. He'd already figured that out for himself.

They looked at each other for a moment longer, and then Carlisle said, 'I guess maybe I judged you wrong, yest'day.'

'You wouldn't be the first.'

'Well, good luck to you,' said Carlisle soberly, offering his hand.

They shook. Hank screamed.

With one final nod, Carlisle scrambled back to O'Neal and the horses, leaving Hennessy to swear silently and shake his head. What he was figuring to do now was madness, not far short of suicide. But he knew he'd never again be able to look at himself in the mirror if he didn't spare Ketchum at least some of the agony to come.

He surveyed the scene below again. One of the Indians was piling loose brush between Ketchum's legs, figuring to scorch his genitals, while another was gesturing to his companions with a knife, asking if it was too soon to separate their captive from his scalp.

Clenching his teeth, Hennessy brought the stock of

the Winchester up to his right shoulder and carefully took aim.

Down below, the Comanche with the knife dropped to his knees, pulled Ketchum's snow-white hair back from his forehead and prepared to make his first cut.

Feeling sick to the stomach, Hennessy pulled the trigger, and a part-second later Ketchum's face exploded, showering the surrounding Indians with blood, brains and bone.

For a moment then there was complete and utter shock. Before the Indians could recover, Hennessy sprang up and started half-falling, half-sliding back down the hill towards his waiting horse. He managed to get a little more than twenty yards before the Indians began to yell and screech in a combination of rage and indignation, and a wild scattering of shots chopped through the brush he'd recently vacated.

The Indians would be scattering for cover now, he thought, certain they were under attack. But it wouldn't take them long to figure out what had really happened, and then they'd come after him, and if they caught him, then he would provide the pleasure he'd just denied them by killing Hank.

That being the case, he had just moments to get as much of a head-start as he could, and he didn't figure to waste a second of it.

He yanked the reins free, threw himself into the saddle and thrust the Winchester back into the scabbard. Then he gave the skittish horse his heels and the animal plunged forward into a flat-out gallop.

A backward glance showed him the first of the

mounted Indians already charging over the top of the rise, and he swore with colour as he urged his horse to greater efforts.

Facing forward again, he saw Carlisle and O'Neal about half a mile ahead of him on the great, sweltering plain, and he swore some more. The fools had gone so far, then reined down to *wait* for him! Damn! He'd given them a chance to get to hell and gone before the Indians came after them, and here they were, throwing it away!

As they started waving him on, he hauled his .45 from its holster, twisted at the waist and loosed off two shots to discourage pursuit, not that he really expected it to do him much good. The Indians knew that his chances of hitting anything from the back of a charging horse were slim at best, and if anything it only made them ride the faster.

The land ahead became a crazy kaleidoscope of yellows, browns and washed-out greens, all of them leaping and falling drunkenly to the lunge and thrust of the charging horse beneath him. But now Hennessy was close enough to bawl at his companions.

'*Ride, damn you!*'

Carlisle and O'Neal, not understanding him, just stayed where they were and continued to wave him on.

He was beyond cursing by now. Seconds later he blurred past the buffalo hunters without even breaking stride, but still yelling for them to *move*, dammit, and at last they got the message and fell in behind him.

Now the choice was so simple that even they could understand it.

They had to ride for their lives . . . or end up fighting for them.

Spooked and trying not to show it, blond-haired, thin-faced Shaun Millican was paying more attention to his surroundings than he was to the four-horse team leaning into the traces ahead of him.

He'd never trusted the Indians, of course, not since his father, a miner from Nevada, had been killed in a Paiute ambush in the Truckee River Valley fourteen years earlier. Shaun, only eight years old at the time, had learned to hate them with a passion after that, and though he would never admit it, he'd learned to fear them, too. After all, his father had been a strong, fit man who'd fought for survival every day of his short life. He was tough, rock-hard, shatterproof, and Shaun had idolized him for it. And yet, that day in early May, the Paiutes had killed him and upwards of fifty men just like him, with little if any loss to their own.

Now, if they could do that, what else were they capable of?

The question had plagued the boy, and thereafter he'd developed an almost morbid interest in Indian affairs. And not just the Paiutes. There was that business with the Sioux in Wyoming a few years later: Captain Jack's Modocs in Oregon; the Apaches in Arizona; the Cheyenne, Arapaho, Caddo and, of course, the worst of the bunch, the Comanches, right here in Texas. Sometimes it seemed there was always Indian trouble some place, and always would be.

For that reason, Shaun had never felt at ease on the

Staked Plains. He'd never quite been able to shake that itchy feeling of being watched: that some invisible foe was forever sizing you up and just waiting for the right moment to chop you down.

He'd never mentioned it to anyone else, of course. He wouldn't dare. They'd have called him seven different kinds of coward to fret for what they considered to be no good reason. But what had befallen Sam Dudley and B. J. Williams the day before had brought back memories of his father's fate and shaken him to the core, and he'd been relieved when Johnny Bourke had announced his decision to haul stakes and head back to Dodge before the price of skins went down.

He shuffled his skinny butt to get more comfortable on the wagon's high seat, suspecting again that Johnny was actually a man after his own heart. As big and jaunty as he was, Johnny had never cared much for the Indians, and just maybe he felt the same way as Shaun – that they could avoid a whole pack of grief by cutting their losses and getting off this Godless high country before hell finally broke loose.

Not that it was going to be easy. They still had a heck of a journey ahead of them, through that wild panhandle country that thrust west from Indian Territory and was known as No Man's Land, but even that was better than being stuck here on the *Llano Estacado*, with an enemy that had no mercy.

Bourke had organized things so that his two wagons were flanked on each side by three outriders. Shaun himself was driving the first vehicle, a one-eyed man called Frank Edgehill at the reins of the second. It had seemed to the short, underweight youngster that the column fairly bristled with guns, but still he continued to scan the scrub-littered, heat-scorched flats around them with that same, nagging combination of fear and dread.

Just then Johnny Bourke, who'd been riding point, drew rein and stiffened, and the fear started biting Shaun with even greater intensity. Immediately he hauled on the reins and stomped on the brake, bringing the wagon to a halt, and Dave Cullen, a buffalo hunter riding a few yards to his right, suddenly sat a little straighter in his saddle and tightened his grip on the .50-calibre rifle balanced across his lap.

For a time then there was only the silence of the plains, punctuated occasionally by the rattle of a chain here, the stamp or blow or head-shake of an impatient horse there, the soft creak of saddle-leather as ill-at-ease men shifted uncomfortably. Then Johnny Bourke, a barrel-chested man with a surprisingly soft voice, turned his horse towards the north-west and gestured, and they all saw it – the thinnest, wispiest spiral of smoke rising skyward about thirty yards away.

Shaun murmured. 'I'll be damned. . . .'

There amid a sea of creosote bush lay a small, temporary encampment occupied by a single white man.

The man, clad in a homespun shirt and blanket leggings, was hunkered beside a small fire with his back to them. His chestnut horse, standing saddled and ready to ride, waited patiently a few yards away. The man must have heard their approach, but gave no sign to acknowledge their presence. Still, that was just about what you'd expect from crazy Milt Hagerman.

Shaun shook his head and let go a soft sigh. He'd never cottoned much to the scalp hunter. Hagerman had a dangerous, unpredictable something about him that made men wary in his presence. Furthermore, it was said around Adobe Walls that he shadowed the Indians real close before making his move against them: that wherever you found him away from the stockade, you could be sure the Indians weren't far distant.

Johnny Bourke walked his horse through the brush towards the camp. Finally Hagerman raised his head and turned to face him. He ran his shining blue eyes from Bourke to the wagons and men waiting behind him on what passed for a trail, and meeting his gaze only with effort, Bourke noted again just how completely the loss of his family had busted and wrecked the last of Hagerman's sanity.

Then he raised his voice, breaking the heavy moment. 'Hagerman! Best you head on back to Adobe Walls before you part company with your hair!'

Hagerman eyed him sinisterly. 'Keep your voice down!' he hissed. 'They're around here somewheres, Johnny-me-boy, an' they ain't deaf! I can feel 'em, an' they're close. So it's your hair they'll be takin', you keep usin' your tonsils at that volume!'

The madman set down the enamel coffee cup he'd been holding and rose to his feet, his sabre knocking gently against his long leg as he bent to scoop up one of his two saddle guns, the Henry repeater, from where it had been leaning against a rock. 'Best you ride on an' ride fast!' he advised.

Bourke licked his bewhiskered lips. 'What about you?'

'I am the avenger,' Hagerman replied, his expression stiff and unmoving, his eyes wide and eerily alive. 'I got a holy task to fulfil.'

'Don't be a fool,' said Bourke. 'Could be you'll get a mite more'n you bargained for today. So show some sense, man! Either come along with us or head back to the stockade.'

Hagerman eyed him from under lowered brows. 'I don't belong in Dodge,' he growled. 'My place is here, on these Staked Plains, carryin' out the Lord's work. Now, git, you son of a dog! They'll be here shortly. I can feel it in my *teeth*.'

And he moved the repeater casually, until the barrel was aimed in Bourke's direction.

Bourke hesitated a moment longer, then spat to the side. 'All right, Milt,' he said gravely. 'I can see you're set on stayin', so I'll leave you to it.'

He backed his horse away from the small camp, took up his position at the head of the column again and then continued scouting the land ahead, leaving the wagons and outriders to move ponderously in his wake. Hagerman watched them go with a hostile twist to his lips, keeping his rifle trained on them until they were out of sight.

They added another mile to their back-trail, then half a mile more, and Johnny Bourke was still thinking about Milt Hagerman and the fate that had broken and reshaped him into something much darker, when an arrow slammed into his horse and sent it toppling to the ground.

Falling with the horse, Johnny just managed to kick out of the stirrups in time to avoid a crushed leg. Rolling, he came back up tearing a pistol from his belt, but an instant later he was knocked backwards by one, two, three, four arrows in the chest, no more than a second between the impact of each one, and he went down again without firing a shot.

Shaun Millican, watching it happen just yards ahead of him, instinctively brought his wagon to a halt, tossed the reins aside and grabbed for the Winchester under his seat. By the time he realized his mistake, that he should have whipped the team to greater speed and tried to reach cover instead, it was too late. The column was stalled at the centre of a narrow basin, unable to go forward or pull back, easy targets for an enemy intent on ambushing them.

A cacophony of wild, piercing war cries was suddenly joined by a fast-moving rumble of hoofs, and when he rose up and twisted sideways with the rifle in his hands, he saw a sizeable band of Indians galloping down on them from a low hill to the north.

Dave Cullen, he saw, was already trying to draw a bead on the approaching Comanches, but finding it difficult because of the frightened horse prancing and swapping ends beneath him.

Then the sky darkened momentarily with another rush of arrows, the feathers with which they'd been fletched giving them a gaudy appearance, like Chinese fireworks at New Year, and Shaun whispered, 'Aw, sweet Jesus. . . .'

Falling back to earth, the barbed tips struck the wagons' sideboards and canvas tops, hit men and horseflesh both, and all at once a new sound was added to the din, that of men and animals screaming in pain and panic.

Seconds later the Indians were among them, spreading chaos and confusion as only Indians could. Men screamed in defiance or agony: guns blasted nearby and far; arrows whipped through the air, occasionally striking flesh with a distinctive, wet thwacking sound, and rideless horses, some carrying their own injuries, began to bolt this way and that, wall-eyed and terrified.

The impact of a bullet fired at close range tore Frank Edgehill off his wagon seat and flung him to the ground. Dave Cullen took a thrown lance in the side and tumbled off his horse, trailing something long and wet and red from the wound. Tearing his gaze away from the dreadful sight, Shaun spotted two warriors charging towards him and worked the long gun's lever in a flustery blur, firing, reloading and firing again.

He caught one of the Comanches in the right shoulder and the brave dropped his hatchet, grabbed for the wound and rode on past, swaying drunkenly in his buffalo-pelt saddle.

That still left the second one, though.

Shaun pumped the combination lever and trigger-guard again, but this time the lever locked fast and a tiny, frightened voice in his mind told him that his inexpert handling had caused the weapon to jam.

Oh God, please, no—

Was this how it had been for his father, he wondered? This sudden, overwhelming rush of blind, bowel-loosening fear coupled with an almost uncontrollable anger at the injustice of it all? Was this how he'd felt when the Paiutes had overwhelmed him and his companions and realization had finally dawned that there was no way out, that this was where it all ended?

Shaun preferred to believe that his father had gone down fighting instead.

Just like *he* was going to do.

With tears stinging his bloodshot blue eyes, he turned the rifle around, figuring to use it as a club, and screamed, '*Come on, then, you sonofabitch! Come on!*'

Eager to take up the challenge, the second Comanche came pounding towards him, but when no more than fifteen feet separated them, someone else blew the bastard's head off his shoulders.

As the head disappeared in a burst of red mist, Shaun knew a giddying moment of shock, disappointment, relief and almost pitiful gratitude. His legs turned rubbery under him and he slumped back onto the wagon seat, his unsteady fingers fumbling instinctively at the trap on the side of the frame to try and clear the jam.

Then, above all the yelling, screaming, gunfire and war cries, he heard a shrill, distinctive cackling. A moment later Milt Hagerman galloped into view, a spiteful smirk twisting at his features, and all at once Shaun realized who had just saved his skin.

115

On his way in, Hagerman caught up the reins of Dave Cullen's milling horse with his free hand and thrust them in the youngster's direction. '*Get outta here!*' he yelled, dodging a tumbling hatchet and using one of his matched Army Colts to shoot the warrior who'd just thrown it. '*Ride an' don't look back!*'

He fired again, this time taking down a knife-wielding brave who had come up on Shaun's blind side and would have skewered him for sure had Hagerman not sent him to hell first.

Scared and confused, Shaun stared into the scalp hunter's face and was startled to see something there that he'd never seen before, a sort of decency and humanity that chased away the madness for just a second, and in that same moment he finally understood that he could do nothing more here, nothing for his companions, nothing to save their cargo, *nothing*.

In any case, there was now precious little fight left to be fought. Most of the men he had hunted and killed and skinned with were already little more than bloodied, unfeeling carcasses themselves.

Without another word he climbed into Cullen's saddle and took the reins, then nodded to Hagerman and lit out as fast as he could. Within seconds he took an arrow in the right calf, the shock of the wound making him sway and slump forward across the horse's neck, but somehow he held on and kept going.

With a grunt of approval, Hagerman promptly dismissed him from mind. After all, he still had Comanches to kill. Dropping from his horse and taking his long guns with him, he threw himself under

116

the brake-locked wagon and set to work, taking aim, leading the target, firing methodically and watching red men die.

For the last week or so, he'd had the strangest feeling. For the first time since everything had gone wrong in his life, he'd started dreaming about his wife and children. Vivid dreams, they were, and good ones too, because it was as if they were telling him that it wouldn't be long now before they were all together again, and that things would be the same as they'd been before.

Something scratched a furrow along Hagerman's right cheek, and hot blood washed down that side of his lean face, but he ignored the wound.

'*Come an' get me, then, you lousy heathens!*' he yelled, switching to the Spencer when the Henry ran dry.

And in the minutes that followed he was a fury of action, firing, killing, firing, wounding, firing, reloading, and it was as if there was nothing the Comanches could do about it. He was unstoppable, absolutely caught up in the slaughter job at hand. . . .

Then, all at once, white-hot pain stabbed through him. He chanced a look down, saw that one of the red devils had managed to catch his left leg with the point of a thrown lance. He screamed once, to relieve the build-up of pain: then, incredibly, he started chuckling again as he set the empty Spencer aside and drew his second Colt.

He had no idea how long he lasted after that.

An arrow hit him in the shoulder. With the softest grunt of pain, Hagerman rolled onto his side, snap-

117

aimed and killed the bowman with a single bullet.

But the Indian's companions used those few scant seconds to charge his position, drag him from cover.

Even now, though, he came out fighting, slashing and thrusting with the only weapon he had left, the cavalry sabre. He took off one brave's fingers, buried the point in another's crotch—

Then one of the Comanches leapt forward and plunged a hatchet blade into his skull.

Just before his brain was cut in two, Hagerman thought, *Mary! It's over now, Mary! I'm comin' home—*

Then it *was* over . . . and he *was* home.

SEVEN

'This damn' waitin's enough to drive a man crazy,' growled Bat Masterson, shaking his head irritably. 'The longer it goes on, the more I reckon the Indians got the lot of 'em.'

Jim McInnery, who was manning one of the low, half-ruined walls to the north-east with Masterson and Oscar Sheppard, spat a mouthful of tobacco juice. 'Anyone ever tell you you're the life an' soul of the party, Bat?' he asked drily.

'I'm only sayin' what we're all thinkin',' Masterson replied.

'Well,' snapped Oscar Sheppard, 'let's just hope we're all wrong.'

And having said his piece, he fell quiet again and thought some more about the calculations they'd made earlier, just after Hennessy, Carlisle and O'Neal had set out after Ketchum's crew. Johnny Bourke's party might have left earlier that same morning, but that still left twenty-eight men at the stockade. That should be enough, he thought, if it came to a fight.

But what if Bat was right, and the Indians *had* accounted for Hank Ketchum and his buddies? That would bring the total down to twenty-five. And if anything happened to Hennessy, Carlisle and O'Neal. . . .

Well, twenty-two looked a darn sight less comforting still.

Making a half-hearted stab at optimism, however, he reminded himself that they were twenty two good men to have beside you in a fight. But when he considered the calibre of the men they might have to go up against, much less their number, it was hard to feel anything but fretful.

McInnery, who'd been staring thoughtfully into the far distance, suddenly frowned as a new thought occurred to him. 'Did Hagerman get back?' he asked.

Sheppard shrugged. 'I never saw him. Maybe the Indians got him, too.'

Masterson shook his head. 'Not Hagerman. He's crazy. Indians wouldn't harm a crazy man.'

'Not even after all he's done to *them*?' Sheppard asked in disbelief.

'Every man has his breakin' point,' muttered McInnery. 'Me, I got no time for Hennessy, but he's right about one thing. The Indians'll only take so much from a man like Hagerman. Crazy or not, they'll swat him good when they've had a bellyful.'

He fell silent then, his attention taken by a spot on the heat-blurred horizon, where a dust cloud could just been seen lifting towards the azure sky. Even as Masterson and Sheppard turned to follow his line of sight, a second, larger dust cloud became visible a short distance behind the first.

'What—?' began Masterson.

'Trouble,' growled McInnery. He pulled an ancient telescope from his buckskins and put it to his eye. A moment later he swore under his breath. 'It's Hennessy and the others!'

Sheppard stiffened. 'You see Ketchum's bunch with 'em?'

'Nope – but I see a pack o' riled-up redskins not far behind 'em!' He heeled towards Masterson. 'Sound the alarm, Bat! We got to give them fellers coverin' fire, else the Indians'll get 'em for sure!'

Bermuda Carlisle hipped around in the saddle and felt the blood drain from his bewhiskered face when he saw just how close the Indians were. Born to the saddle, the Comanches and their Arapaho allies had steadily closed the gap with their quarry. Now only a quarter-mile separated the pursuers from the pursued.

He faced front again, shook his head and spat. It had been a nightmare flight, and it had pushed the white men and their mounts to the edge of their endurance. He'd hoped the Indians might give up after the first couple of miles, and to his relief they *did*, once. For some reason that wasn't immediately obvious, they'd reined down, clustered together, and a couple of them had pointed northward.

Slowing his own mount, Carlisle had chanced a look that way, seen black smoke billowing skyward. He didn't know what it meant, and right then was in no position to guess, but just before Hennessy yelled for him to keep moving, it occurred to him that the smoke was coming from the direction Johnny Bourke would have taken to get back to Dodge.

Then he, Hennessy and O'Neal were pushing forward again, and their foam-flecked, wild-eyed horses were giving them all they could.

And the Indians started coming after them again.

Times like that, a man thinks about all kinds of things, but mostly he asks himself questions. What's going to happen to him? Is he going to get out of this? What can he do to turn the tables on the men who plan to do him down? He wonders if he led a good life or whether it could have stood a little improvement, and almost inevitably he remembers his family and asks himself whatever became of them after he moved on and they lost touch—

Not wanting to pursue that line of thought any more, Carlisle tightened his jaw, faced front again – and frowned. Distracted though he was, the flats across which they had just started racing looked oddly familiar to him. And in the same moment something half a mile ahead and a little to his right claimed his attention. Recognizing it, he let go a strange sound that was half-exclamation and half-sob, and thought, with a disbelieving kind of wonder, *Adobe Walls! Adobe Walls, dammit! Christ Almighty, we're gonna make it after all!*

That was when his horse went out from under him.

By the greatest ill-fortune the animal stepped into a prairie-dog hole, and with a loud cracking of bone crashed forward, mane over tail. Carlisle himself was flung in a wide arc, hit the ground hard and rolled, once, twice, maybe a dozen times.

He knew he was finished for sure, then. He staggered back to his feet, the world spinning before his half-glazed eyes, and stumbled towards the horse, intending to make a grab for his heavy buffalo gun. At the same moment he heard hoof beats behind him, coming fast and rapidly growing louder.

As he turned around, Hennessy drew level with him, hauled rein, drew his Colt and took aim. Carlisle stared up at him, the breath stuck in his tortured throat. Is this how it went, then, when a man had no hope of rescue? A man like Hennessy came along and shot him dead?

Carlisle's eyes went wide as Hennessy fired the gun, and it was a long few seconds before he realized that Hennessy had been aiming at the fallen horse, determined to put the creature out of its misery while he still could.

Then Hennessy was shoving the weapon away, kicking one foot out of the near-side stirrup and shoving his left hand down toward him. '*Come on!*'

Knowing it was crazy to do so, Carlisle shook his head. 'That nag won't get far, carryin' double!'

Hennessy bawled, 'We ain't got the time to argue about it!'

'*Then git!*'

Hennessy told him what he'd told him earlier. 'Your choice.'

Time seemed to suspend itself then, as they looked at each other, with the sound of hard-running Indian ponies and throat-scraping war cries growing closer behind them.

At last Carlisle moved. He toed in, grabbed Hennessy's wrist and swung up behind him, and seconds later the horse, gamely carrying double the burden, started ploughing back towards the settlement.

Arrows zipped after them through the late afternoon air, and the screeching yips and cries of the blood-hungry Indians sounded as if they were coming from right behind them. Hennessy's horse suddenly stumbled under the double weight and Carlisle shouted, 'I told you we wouldn't get far!'

Hennessy bawled, 'Shut up!' He didn't have the wind to say any more.

The horse righted itself again, kept going. And now there came a new sound into the mix – a sudden, angry volley of rifle fire.

Alerted by Bat Masterson, buffalo hunters had answered the call to give the newcomers the covering fire they so desperately needed. Two Indians flew backwards off their horses. Another Indian snapped his neck when one .50-calibre slug ripped through his horse and the animal went down, throwing him.

Then O'Neal, followed by Hennessy and Carlisle, ran their winded mounts through the crumbling fortifications and into the relative safety of Adobe Walls itself, and more or less poured themselves out of their saddles to stand weak-legged and gasping for air in front of Hanrahan's saloon.

As if by mutual consent, the assembled buffalo hunters gave the distant Indians another fusillade just as

Billy Dixon and Mike Welch appeared in Hennessy's line of sight and ushered all three of them into the saloon. 'By God,' breathed Billy, 'you fetched a peck o' trouble with you! But I'm glad t' see you in one piece, Cal.'

'I'm glad to *be* in one piece.'

'Ketchum's crew?' asked Mike.

Hennessy shook his head. 'We were too late.'

'They're retreatin'!' Bat Masterson yelled from outside.

Hennessy leaned against the counter and closed his eyes. That figured. The Indians wouldn't like the odds now, nor the fact that their enemies had better cover than they did. But this thing was going to get worse before it got better. The Indians would try their luck again, sooner or later.

He heard Jim McInnery yelling for the others to cease fire and save their ammunition. A few moments later Adobe Walls fell absolutely silent but for the furious barking of the Scheidler brothers' Newfoundland dog.

He opened his eyes again to find Bermuda Carlisle staring at him. The stocky little man was sporting an angry bump on his forehead, an injury he'd picked up when he fell from his horse. 'Reckon I'd've been finished for sure if you hadn't come back for me,' he said in his low, gravelly voice. 'I'm obliged.'

Hennessy just nodded.

Billy and Mike, meanwhile, were already thinking ahead. Going back to the doorway, Billy called out, 'All right, you men, come gather round!'

All but Jim McInnery and Bat Masterson came in to

listen to what he had to say. They stayed outside to make sure the Indians didn't come back. The rest of the men, their blood still up from the recent action, wanted to enjoy their moment of triumph, but Billy had other ideas.

'That wasn't much of a scrap,' he began. 'Wasn't even big enough to be called a skirmish. But it was sure as hell a taste of what's still to come.'

He eyed them all, his expression bleak. 'Hank an' them other fellers Cal went to warn, they're dead. That makes six of us the Indians have accounted for since yest'day – that's to say, six we know about. So if they're aimin' to get us good an' mad, they're doin' quite a job of it.'

Mike took over. 'But we ain't gonna oblige 'em, you men. Hear me? We might hate 'em, and we may hanker to kill 'em to even things up a little. But we ain't gonna lose our heads over this. We can't afford to. We got to stay calm, let *them* make all the mistakes!'

'Let 'em come!' yelled a man in the crowd. 'They'll find gunpower an' lead awaitin' 'em!'

As a cheer rose up from the others, Hennessy thought bleakly, *So will we, mister.*

So will we.

With a heavy heart, Quanah Parker watched his men return to camp and wished there had been more of them. And as he listened to the wailing of the squaws who had all too suddenly become widows, he told himself that, at such a price, today's victory could hardly be called a victory at all.

The stern line of his mouth grew tighter still as his hooded eyes moved toward Isatai's *tipi*. Had Isatai not said they would be invulnerable to the white man's bullets? Why, then, had the magic of the Sacred Powers deserted them? Had he, Quanah, done something to displease them? Or had there been something false to Isatai's claims all along?

It was, he thought, quite likely. And yet there was the evidence of his own eyes to consider. Eagle Hand had fired a pistol at Isatai, and Isatai's magic had made the bullet fall harmlessly to the dust. This he had seen for himself.

He could see also by the triumphant smiles on the faces of Eagle Hand, Windwalker and the others that they shared none of his misgivings. All that mattered to them was that they had finally struck back, and that it was good to have done so.

'Our people have made a fine start, Quanah,' said Satanta, coming to stand beside him. 'And yet your expression is one of sorrow. Why do you not celebrate?'

'Because I think of those brothers whose faces I shall not see again,' Quanah replied simply.

Satanta shook his head. 'You think too much, my friend. Sometimes it is all you do. You say you lead the Kwahadis, and yet most of the time you do not lead them at all, but leave such matters to the likes of Isatai. You should take command, as you did when first you sought to burn the white man's stockade to the ground!'

Quanah turned on the Kiowa so fast that Satanta flinched, and Lone Wolf, standing nearby, quickly hurried over to prevent a confrontation. 'I wish no strife with you,' Quanah said in a low hiss, addressing himself to Satanta. ''You are a guest here, an *honoured* guest. But to take such a tone with me does you no honour. You do not take another man's hospitality and then fire words like arrows to injure him.'

'That was not my intent,' Satanta replied stiffly.

'Nevertheless those words *do* injure,' said Quanah. 'And for that reason you would be wise not to speak them again.'

The returning warriors slid from their horses, enjoying their moment. Only then did Isatai appear from the smoky darkness of his *tipi*. He was completely naked and, as usual, had daubed his skeletal frame from top to toe with ochre-yellow paint.

As a crowd began to gather around him, he called in a solemn voice, 'I welcome you home, my brave warriors! You have struck a mighty blow this day! But I see that not all of those warriors who rode out this morning have returned, and this saddens my heart, because it tells me that those who died chose not to believe the assurances of the gods!'

Hearing that, Quanah stepped forward with a frown. 'What is that you say, Isatai?' he demanded.

Isatai turned to face him, as if only now becoming aware of his presence. 'It is a question of belief, my chief,' he explained glibly, still loud enough for his audience to hear. 'These men – Eagle Hand, Windwalker and all the others you see here before you – they believed the word of the gods and trusted in them . . . and so they have returned, whole and unharmed.'

'And the rest?'

'Doubters,' Isatai replied regretfully. 'They showed *no* belief, *no* trust, and were punished for it.'

Quanah opened his mouth to debate that, but instead said nothing. To argue with the shaman now would be to set his people even harder against him, for the gods and those who spoke for them held more sway than did he, a mere half-breed. He dare not call Isatai's words into question, and they both knew it.

Turning his back on Quanah, and dismissing him with the gesture, Isatai once again addressed the crowd. 'This is but the beginning of a great victory for our people,' he said. 'We will strike again and again, until we have driven the hated white man from our lands! This the Sacred Powers have foretold!'

As a cheer went up from Isatai's audience, Quanah was reminded yet again that Isatai was a man who would sooner lead than counsel. And again he remembered Satanta's recent criticism. *You say you lead the Kwahadis, and yet most of the time you do not lead them at all, but leave such matters to the likes of Isatai.* He saw now that Satanta had spoken only the truth.

It was clear, then, that this was the time to lead, or have that leadership taken from him by another.

On impulse he stepped forward, and almost immediately the yipping and cheering faded to near silence. Isatai glanced at him, fury at the interruption showing briefly in his sunken eyes, until he lowered his head and took a deferential pace backward.

'Tomorrow.' Quanah said slowly, 'before the rising of the sun, we will take the battle to the white man at

129

the place he calls Adobe Walls. We will kill all of his number there and by the time we are finished there will be nothing left to say that such a place ever existed! And if more white men dare to invade our lands, we will kill them also! White men, Yellow-Legs, we will wage war on them all until we are victorious – and I will lead you to that victory!'

Once again the assembly erupted in a roar. Quanah's words were greeted by the enthusiastic yip and screech of war cries, the waving of lance and bow and rifle and hatchet, and Isatai, trying gamely to mask his true feelings, could not quite hide the fact that he hated the adulation his chief was now receiving.

Quanah turned and walked back to Satanta and Lone Wolf, his shoulders squared, his chest out-thrust, his heart pounding. Regarding both men, he said, 'Are you with us, my friends?'

Satanta and Lone Wolf exchanged a brief, excited glance, after which Satanta nodded. 'We are with you, my brother. We are with you!'

Billy Dixon pulled the half-smoked quirley from his mouth and flung it away in disgust. The strong Spanish tobacco usually soothed him, but not today. Today there was no soothing to be had.

'An' that's another thing,' he grumbled. 'If them redskins want to mix it up, that's fine. We'll mix it with 'em. But why drag it out? Why not come an' let's get to it?' Then, hearing himself, he quirked a sour smile at his companion. 'Aw, hell. Much more of this an' I'll be as crazy as Hagerman.'

Around them the stockade was quiet in the fading daylight, and those men not assigned to keeping watch on the plains beyond the patched walls were mourning their dead in the saloon, mess-hall or barracks.

'This thing had to come to a head sooner or later,' Hennessy pointed out softly.

'Sure, sure,' replied Billy. 'An' you knew it all along. That's why you quit the business, ain't it?'

Hennessy looked off across the desert. It looked so lonely, but he couldn't help wondering just how empty it really was. 'It was always a lousy job,' he said after a moment. 'But it paid well, and we were killing for a reason. We put meat into folks' bellies and fur coats on their backs. But somewhere along the way all that changed. Easterners started killing the buffalo for sport. *Sport,* for God's sake! Men like you and me were hired to kill 'em just to spite and deprive the Indians. We weren't hunters after that, Billy, we was just plain murderers.'

'I don't call it murder to kill a buffalo.'

'No. But watching the Indians starve to death because we killed or spoilt all their meat, watching their women get so weak they couldn't feed their young 'uns, destroying them that slow, hard way . . . *that* was murder.'

Billy frowned. 'But they're only Indians.'

Hennessy shook his head in disgust. 'By Christ,' he said. 'You *still* don't get it, do you? They live, they love, they laugh, they cry, they die, Billy. They do all the things *we* do. We even bleed the same colour. They're *us,* damn you, and we're *them.* The sooner folks on

131

both sides get that into their skulls, the better off we'll *all* be.'

Billy made no immediate comment, because he knew, deep down, that Hennessy was right. 'So you came to see me for old times' sake and ended up gettin' stuck in the middle of all this,' he murmured. 'I'm sorry about that, I truly am. This isn't your fight, amigo, but you've got to fight it anyway.'

'Not if the soldiers get here first.'

'That's a big if,' Billy replied. 'Got to rely on Bourke an' his party gettin' through to Dodge first, an' from what Bermuda Carlisle tells me, that doesn't look too likely.'

'Well, let's hope they make it, or sure as hell we're on our own,' said Hennessy, thinking, *On our own – against God knows how many blood-hungry bucks.*

'I'm gonna try for some sleep,' Billy mumbled. 'Might not get a chance tomorrow.' He nodded towards a solitary figure standing watch behind another section of broken wall thirty yards away. 'If you're still in the mood for talk, why not talk to him? I reckon he could stand it.'

Hennessy raised his eyebrows. 'Masterson?'

'I know you ain't got much time for him, Cal, but he's not a bad 'un, once you get to know him, an' he's a damn' fine shot, maybe even a match for you!'

'He's still wet behind the ears, Billy, and he's got a lot of growing up to do. If he lives long enough, he's going to do most of it in the next twenty-four hours.'

'Well, let's hope he does,' Billy answered. ' 'Cause he's a good young feller, Cal. Given the chance, he'll make an even better man.'

While Billy headed for the barracks, Hennessy ghosted across to Masterson's position. Hearing him come, Masterson turned his head and offered a subdued greeting.

'Mind some company?' asked Hennessy.

Masterson looked surprised by the question. 'Please yourself.'

'I'll leave you be, if you'd prefer.'

He looked into Masterson's eyes, barely visible now in the growing gloom, and tried to decide just how things were with the boy. He was scared, that was for certain. Scared and trying to hide it, just like the rest of them.

'No, that's all right.'

'Good. 'Cause I reckon there's been a little ill-feeling between us, and it's about time we cleared it up.'

'Oh?'

Hennessy nodded. 'I'll say it plain, Bat. You're a kid. A know-nothing, wet-behind-the-ears kid. You look at things, but you don't really see 'em. You listen to what people say, but you don't really hear 'em. You're young, and you think you already know all the answers. But I got news for you, boy.'

Masterson had stiffened. 'What's that?'

'They can't hang you for it. It's how we all start off. The smart ones eventually wise up and start to pay attention. The rest . . . well, they don't usually last too long.'

'An' which kind do you suppose I am?'

'Billy speaks highly of you, and Billy's a good judge of men.'

'Then Lord help me if I let him down,' Masterson muttered before he could stop himself. He gave Hennessy a furtive glance and added belligerently, 'Not that I'm scared!'

'We're all scared, Bat. I sure am. But when push comes to shove, I'll stand my ground and do what has to be done – and I got a feeling you'll do the same.'

'Why?'

'Because as far as I can see, the only thing you're missing right now is experience. The rest of it – honour, decency, loyalty, courage . . . those things you've already got.'

Masterson shrugged. 'I appreciate the sentiment,' he said awkwardly, 'but I didn't need to be told that.'

'Then I'm sorry if I spoke out of turn,' Hennessy apologized, and made to turn away.

'Hennessy,' Masterson called.

The taller man turned back.

Masterson said sheepishly, 'I'm a lousy liar, Hennessy. I reckon I did need to hear that, and I'm obliged.' Abruptly he thrust out his right hand. 'Best if we started over again, huh?'

'Why not?'

They shook, and the night wore on.

Mounted astride his favourite spotted pony, Quanah stared across the stark, moon-silvered plain ahead. Behind him came Satanta and Lone Wolf, then Isatai, and behind them Eagle Hand and Windwalker and score upon score of Comanche, Kiowa and Cheyenne warriors, more even than the days in two whole years.

Eyes half-closed, Isatai was murmuring ancient invocations in a monotone, the words of which had been passed down to him by his grandfather. The sound of it filled the trotting warriors with confidence and anticipation, as they too kept watch on the distant horizon.

Battle was coming, and with it the chance for honour, glory and revenge. But only Quanah seemed aware that there was also the chance for death – maybe death for many of them.

Not that he was scared for himself. But he feared for the loss of his men, for the heartache and hardship it would bring to their families. Victory over the whites would be cold comfort indeed to a grieving squaw and her now-fatherless children.

However, his mind was set. Nothing would stop the violence to come this day. And it was just possible that the gods would protect them, as Isatai had foretold: that against all the odds Isatai himself really was speaking with a straight tongue.

No more than two or three hill slopes separated them from Adobe Walls when Quanah finally signalled a halt. Wordlessly, his men dismounted and led their ponies the rest of the way, moving softer than ever now, determined that the whites should not learn of their presence until the last possible moment.

Quanah's heart began to beat even faster. His people had burned Adobe Walls down once before. He saw now that he should never have allowed the whites to come back and establish such a firm foothold in this *Llano Estacado* country again.

An excited mutter ran through his men. Ahead lay

the ghostly silhouette of the place they had come to destroy, a quiet, dark series of half-fallen walls and squat, stout buildings covered in shadow.

Turning, Quanah told his men to make ready. This at last was the hour when they lived or died, won or lost. The hour when white man and red would fight to the death in the battle for Adobe Walls.

EIGHT

Sometime around two in the morning a sudden, dry cracking sound ripped through the silence. In the stillness of the night it sounded even louder than it actually was.

Already jumpy, the occupants of Adobe Walls came awake within seconds, Hennessy no exception. Grabbing the Winchester he'd left under his bunk, he came up out of his blankets and ran outside, fully-clothed. In the chill moonlight he saw men in various stages of undress racing southeast from the hide yard and followed them, expecting the worst. The Newfoundland dog was among them somewhere, yapping his fool head off.

About halfway to Jimmy Hanrahan's saloon they met a handful of hide men coming from the opposite direction. Someone – Hennessy thought it was Isaac Scheidler – called urgently, 'Vat iss it, vat's wrong?'

California Joe Milner said, 'Damn' ridgepole in Jimmy's saloon snapped. Like to've brought the roof down, but I think we got it.'

A couple of men near Hennessy swore at the false

alarm, a couple more sagged in relief, but yet another suggested they go on to Hanrahan's, finish roping the ridgepole back together and have a drink or two while they were at it. The idea met with a fair deal of approval.

'I'm of a different mind,' said Masterson, stopping them all in their tracks. 'You ask me, I say we'd do better to keep clear heads.'

Watching him, Hennessy thought, *Well, damn me if the kid isn't starting to show sense at last.*

Jacob Scheidler, a big man with a long, unruly brown beard, was inclined to agree. '*Ja.* I sleep vile I get the chance, I think.' And together with the dog, he and his brother turned and headed back towards their wagon.

Billy Dixon glanced at Mike Welch. 'What do you reckon?' he asked quietly.

Mike shrugged. 'Just watch how much you fellers imbibe, you hear me?'

Satisfied with the response, the hunters began to disperse, some to head for the saloon, others – including Billy, Mike and Bermuda Carlisle – to scare up some coffee at Charlie Rath's store. Mike had only gone a few yards, however, when he realized that the recent commotion had disturbed the horses grazing beyond the larger of the two hide yards. Hearing the sounds they made milling uneasily, he peered around until he spotted a lean young man by the name of Billy Ogg. 'Best you go fetch them nags in off the meadow, Billy,' he said.

Ogg gave a brief salute. 'Ayuh. I'll see to it.'

He turned and trotted off into the darkness.

Hennessy himself was about to head back to the barracks when he noticed William Olds and his wife standing a few yards away. In his haste, Olds had clawed on a pair of black pants and thumbed the suspenders up over a creased undershirt. His wife was almost lost in a voluminous dressing-gown that was buttoned to the throat. She was clutching her man's arm, the eyes in her pale, fleshy face darting fearfully at every shadow. Neither one seemed to know what to do for the best, and nor could Hennessy blame them, for trouble wasn't just coming any more, it was almost *here*. he could feel it.

Olds, noticing him, offered a distracted nod, then made to guide his wife back to their quarters behind the eatery. They were an amiable, devoted couple, and Hennessy had liked them from the start. On impulse he called Olds's name, and the heavy-set man stopped and came over to him, a frown on his big, pleasant face.

'Yes, Mr Hennessy?'

Hennessy was momentarily lost for words. Then he said awkwardly, 'If there's trouble tomorrow . . . well, you and your wife, you just find yourselves a safe place and keep your heads down. Rest of us'll do all the fighting.'

Olds shook his head. 'Oh, I couldn't allow that, Mr Hennessy. Reckon I'll stand my ground, same as you.'

'And get yourself killed in the process?'

'Not if I can help it, sir, no.'

Hennessy sighed. 'When was the last time you used a weapon, Olds?'

139

'It's been a while, I grant you.'

'Well, me and the rest of these men use 'em every day, so leave the fighting to us. Besides,' and here his eyes flickered briefly toward Mrs Olds, who was watching them curiously from a distance of maybe five yards, 'you've got responsibilities.'

Olds nodded again. 'That I have. She's all I got, an' all I've ever wanted. An' that's why I reckon I'll do everything in my power to protect her.'

Hennessy looked him straight in the eye and saw that there'd be no arguing with him. 'Well, watch yourself, then,' he counselled softly. 'When it starts, don't lose your head or get impatient. Just find good cover, take your time and pick your targets.'

'I'll do that, don't fret.'

As Olds went back to his wife, Hennessy turned to watch the men making their way towards the saloon, where lamplight was now filling the greasy tarpaper windows. Was it likely they'd heed Big Mike's words and watch how much they drank this night? He didn't think so.

He brought the Winchester up across his shoulder and was just about to continue on his way towards the barracks when he sensed a sudden rush of movement off to his left.

A split second later Billy Ogg came racing back out of the darkness.

'*Indians!*' he yelled. '*Indians! They're here!*'

They came as if out of nowhere, hundreds upon hundreds of warriors strung out in a series of loose, screaming ranks. Quanah was in the lead, Isatai right beside him.

Seeing Isatai in so prominent a position made Quanah wonder fleetingly if perhaps he had misjudged the holy man after all. But then Isatai was forgotten as he heeled his horse on through the hated stockade, and a white man appeared in his path.

Quanah saw his bloodless, fear-slack face and wide, startled eyes with tremendous clarity. Then he hurled his lance overarm, and the projectile smashed through the man's sternum and threw him backwards.

Second to die was a hunter named Tyler. The sudden, terrifying racket of the attacking Indians had frozen him in his tracks, but by the time he snapped out of it and broke into a run, it was too late. A .44 bullet slammed through his left lung. An arrow skewered his neck and another bullet whacked him in the chest. He went down in a heap.

Hennessy saw it happen from a distance of less than twenty yards, swung the Winchester down off his shoulder, braced the weapon against his hip and loosed off a shot that caught a charging Kiowa in the shoulder and punched him back off his mount.

Another Indian galloped in, screaming for all he was worth. He tried to cave Hennessy's head in with a hatchet but missed and went on past. Hennessy turned, tracked him, waited a moment, then fired again. The slug ripped a fist-sized hole out of the Comanche's spine and flung him forward, over his horse's neck.

As the Indians continued to swarm between the walls and buildings, some of them throwing flaming torches

141

at anything that might catch fire, the Scheidler brothers, Isaac and Jacob, leapt from their wagon with the
Newfoundland going crazy around their feet.

Cursing in German, Isaac Scheidler raised his Henry
.45/.70 and shot a Kiowa off his horse. He was reloading when he heard his brother, somewhere off to his
left, yell a warning.

Isaac turned just as a mounted Cheyenne ran him
through with a long, feathered lance. The force of the
impact was such that it rammed the weapon straight
through his stomach and out of his back. The big
German went stiff as a board, then collapsed.

Incensed, the Newfoundland dog went blurring
after the Cheyenne and with one muscular bound
managed to grab the Indian by his ankle. The
Cheyenne tried to kick him loose, lost his balance
instead and tumbled from the saddle. By the time he
regained his feet and made a grab for the hatchet at his
waist, the dog was on him again, displaying a savagery
it had never shown before. The Cheyenne didn't last
long after that.

With tears streaking his big, jowly face, Jacob
Scheidler cocked and fired his Model 1866 Winchester
again and again, blowing Indians away to left and right
as he half-stumbled, grief-stricken, straight into the
charging horde. Only a sudden bristling of arrows in
his barrel chest finally stopped him dead.

Bermuda Carlisle, meanwhile, dragged a Richards/
Mason conversion Colt .44 from his belt and threw a
couple of wild shots into the darkness, then started
running for the saloon. An arrow blurred past his

head, clipping his right ear, and the second he clutched at the wound, his palm filled with blood.

He twisted just as a Kiowa in a small fur turban and a grease-stained hide shirt leapt from his horse and came at him in a flat-out run, hatchet in one hand, circular shield in the other and thrust out before him.

Carlisle shot at him and saw dust fly from the shield where the bullet struck, but still the Kiowa kept coming. Then a deeper boom filled the night, and a moment later a ragged hole was torn through the shield, the bullet that made it ripping on into the torso behind it. As the Indian was literally tossed aside, Carlisle spun to face his benefactor.

Bat Masterson paused in the act of reloading his Big Fifty to throw him a grim salute.

As Hennessy levered in another reload, he realized that Olds and his wife, stunned by the appearance of the Indians, were still clutching each other nearby. '*Come on!*' he bawled. As if waking from a dream. Olds lumbered into motion, dragging his wife along in his wake.

Hennessy made straight for the nearest building, O'Keefe's smithy, but it wasn't easy. The Indians were everywhere now, most still mounted but a fair number afoot, yelling their excitement and firing guns and bows almost indiscriminately at anything still moving.

They were almost to their destination when Mrs Olds suddenly cried out. Hennessy spun, saw a Comanche on foot racing at him with a lance thrust forward at waist height. The brave was young, not even twenty, slim but tight-muscled, with long hair worn in otterskin drops and what appeared to be a recently broken nose. In that one passing moment Hennessy had the damnedest feeling that he knew the man, but—

In the same moment it came to him that this was Tahkay, the hot-headed brave who'd fought with him in the arroyo where he'd found Dudley and Williams a short lifetime before; he pulled the trigger and blew a hole in the Indian's belly. Tahkay went down and kicked for a moment, then died.

Seeing it happen, Mrs Olds came close to collapse. Only her husband, cradling her protectively in his big arms, kept her on her feet. Hennessy hurried around to the woman's other side, hooked an arm beneath hers and together they half-dragged, half-propelled her on towards O'Keefe's.

Next moment they were at the smithy's big double doors, and Hennessy was hammering at the rough wood and yelling to be let inside. One of the doors opened a fraction and Hennessy put his free hand on Olds's back and shoved the pair of them to safety ahead of him. Oscar Sheppard and a couple of other men were already there. Sheppard quickly dragged the big door shut and dropped the bar in place.

Hennessy sucked in a steadying breath, threw himself down beside one of the smithy's small, unglazed windows. A brief glance told him he was sharing the place with Tom O'Keefe and Jim McInnery in addition to Sheppard. As near as he could see, most of the other hide men had also made it to cover and were split about equally between Hanrahan's saloon and

Charlie Rath's store. The lights in the saloon had been doused, the windows busted so that the men inside could return fire at their attackers.

A few small fires had taken hold of the parked wagons. The flames spilled, darting amber shadows across the body-littered stockade. As he watched, all but one of the Indians vanished into the darkness, their first attack over. The Comanche who decided to linger was bare-ass naked and daubed with yellow paint. Defiantly he trotted his horse back and forth before the defenders, making all manner of obscene gestures to accompany his bellowed insults.

Hennessy quickly recognized the shaman for what he was, and drew a bead on him. Kill a man like this and you achieved two things – you demoralized the enemy and put some heart back into your own side. But marksman though he was, his aim let him down this time, and once the holy man had finished mocking and jeering, he retreated without so much as a scratch on him.

'How're you fellers fixed for weapons and ammunition?' Hennessy asked when the shaman finally vanished from sight.

Tom O'Keefe said, 'We'll manage, just about. It was a good thing that ridgepole broke when it did, otherwise them Indians would've had us cold.'

'You got a spare rifle, Mr O'Keefe?' asked Olds.

'Here. Maybe you can help reload for us, Mrs Olds? If things get a little wild?'

The woman, pulling herself together with effort,

managed a shaky nod.

Then the lull was over, and the Indians were turning from their initial charge to make a second pass.

Tightening his grip on the Winchester, Hennessy snapped through clenched teeth, '*Look lively. you men! Here they come again!*'

In the store, Billy Dixon was yelling much the same thing.

He'd been lucky to reach Rath's place in one piece. While he was still racing for cover, a Cheyenne had appeared alongside him and thrown himself from his mount onto Billy's back. They'd struggled for a while, the Cheyenne doing his best to burn Billy's face off with the flaming torch he'd been carrying, but somehow Billy had wriggled free, regained his feet and clawed his Remington from leather.

He'd shot the Cheyenne in the side and the sonofabitch had gone down, dropping the flickering torch as he grabbed for the wound. But his fighting blood was still up, and ignoring the pain he'd launched himself at Billy again.

As they crashed to the ground for a second time, the Remington had spun from Billy's fingers. Next thing he knew, the Cheyenne had him by the throat and was throttling the life out of him, and there didn't seem to be a whole lot he could do about it.

Then, in casting around for the fallen Remington, his right hand had closed upon the handle of the flaming torch instead, and he'd brought it up and shoved it hard against the side of the Cheyenne's head. The

Cheyenne had lurched sideways, screaming as he tried desperately to smother his burning hair and ear. Billy had stumbled away from him, reclaimed his .44 and put a second bullet in the brave's belly to finish him for good.

But now the bastards were back, coming fast and throwing everything they had against them. Indians sprang from their mounts to pound against doors and shuttered windows with rifle-butts and tomahawks. The noise was as deafening as it was unnerving. Others tried to break the doors in by backing their horses into them. In the smithy, Hennessy drew his Colt, shoved it through the window and, turning it to the left, triggered three blind shots. A moment later, the Indian trying that particular manoeuvre squealed and dropped from his horse, clutching his blood-stained chest. The warrior's wall-eyed mount surged off into the darkness.

'I'm empty!' yelled William Olds, turning from his own window and thrusting his borrowed Henry repeater to his wife, who was down on her knees behind him, surrounded by the few boxes of cartridges O'Keefe had managed to scare up.

She took the Henry. It seemed to weigh a ton in her small hands. Doing her best to control the trembling of her fingers, she set about feeding .44-calibre rimfire cartridges into the breech, one, two, three. . . .

She'd known trouble was brewing, of course. No one could say they hadn't been warned. Not one of them had any right to be here. They were trespassers, lawbreakers, and now they were paying the price. But who had there ever been to turn them out? The army rarely showed itself in these parts. So Charlie Rath and the others – Charlie Myers, Fred Leonard, Tom O'Keefe and Jimmy Hanrahan – had come out here after the hide men, figuring to make good money, and she and her beloved William had come with much the same intention.

But they hadn't been looking to get rich quick. All they'd wanted was enough of a stake to start an eatery in Dodge, a fine, friendly place where the food was good and the customers appreciated the white iron-stone dishes upon which it was served, and which had been imported all the way from England.

'*Darn it, woman! Reload!*'

William's voice, carrying such uncharacteristic anger, made her flinch. He was normally such a quiet, patient man. But, of course, this was neither the time nor the place for peace or patience.

She finished reloading the Henry, called her husband's name and lifted the weapon towards him. '*Here, William. Be careful!*'

Panicky now, Olds turned at the waist, grabbed the rifle by its barrel and tried to pull it from her grasp – unaware that her right index finger was still curled around the brass trigger.

The Henry went off with a roar that drowned Olds's cry. The bullet smashed up through his chin and burst out the top of his head, spraying gore everywhere. Again she screamed. '*William!*'

Beyond hearing, Olds dropped to the packed-earth floor beside her. That he had died almost instantly was and would remain little comfort to his stunned widow. All that mattered right then was that her husband was dead – *and, dear God, that she had killed him.*

The attack lasted maybe ten or fifteen minutes more, though it seemed a hell of a lot longer. Then the Indians turned and retreated back into the darkness. They did not return.

After a time, Oscar Sheppard whispered, 'It's over.'

But it wasn't.

The Indians hit them again about an hour later, and *kept* hitting them, off and on, for the next three days.

Three days. . . .

Seventy-two hours spent watching and waiting, with little or no water to slake a man's thirst; of being cooped up in the saloon or the store or the smithy as the hard June sun hammered down and turned each building into an oven; of sharing space with the dead and having to listen to the sufferings of the wounded; of hearing Mrs Olds alternately weeping softly and asking her Lord for forgiveness and knowing there was nothing you could do or say that would ever make her feel any easier about what had happened.

There were great long stretches when nothing stirred and nothing happened. All the trapped hide men could do was watch and wait and starve and thirst and try to fight their gritty-eyed fatigue. Then the Indians were there again, this mix of blood-hungry Comanche, Kiowa and Cheyenne, as if from out of nowhere, sniping from a distance at first, to keep the defenders' heads down, then right up close on horseback, hurling lance and hatchet through shattered windows and patched-up doorways, determined to pick off as many whites as they could.

It was in those moments that Hennessy and the other men came to life, when it was kill or be killed and there was no longer any time just to sit and ponder and try to ignore the all-too-obvious hopelessness of their situation.

Those sudden bursts of violence broke the monotony of just waiting to die. But for some, they brought death all the sooner. During one attack, Jim McInnery caught a hatchet in the face, made a strange combination of scream and gurgle, then staggered back, arms and legs twitching, until at last he stiffened, dropped and lay still.

The Indians suffered casualties too, of course. Out in the open, they made good targets by day, and the withering fire directed at them from Billy and the other men in Rath's store, and those like Masterson and Carlisle and Mike Welch in the saloon, claimed braves and their mounts in about equal measure. Soon the area around Adobe Walls was littered with bodies, most of them red.

But there was no sense of triumph in the buffalo hunters. With little or no water to be had and their ammunition slowly but surely dwindling, they had to be content with simply staying alive, always in the hope that the Indians would give up, which was none too likely, or that someone would get through to Dodge and bring help – which seemed equally doubtful.

After dark, things grew even worse. The Indians

could creep in close and hammer on the doors and shutters to keep their enemies awake and on edge. Once they tried to set fire to the smithy, but Hennessy and Oscar Sheppard managed to kill the Comanches and stamp out the flames before they could do much damage. But of course, it all served to wear them down, and by the morning of the third day spirits were low and tempers were short.

Hennessy sat at his small window, surrounded by spent cartridges, with the stink of the dead and the sharp tang of spent powder heavy in his nostrils, and tried to put himself in the Indians' moccasins and imagine what they might do next. This thing hadn't gone well for them. Losses had been high. And it wasn't in their nature to starve the enemy out. They preferred quick victories, not the kind of drawn-out siege into which this particular affair had turned.

He was still considering the Indians' options when he heard a sound off to the south-west. He stiffened, moved a little closer to the window and glanced outside. O'Keefe, noticing him, hustled over in a half-crouch, rifle clamped hard in his hands.

'What is it?' he asked. 'What's happenin'?'

'It's Billy.'

'Billy?'

'The crazy sonofabitch's left the store. He's looking around.'

'What the hell does he think he's playin' at?'

Hennessy made a quick, concerned scan of their seemingly empty surroundings. 'I think he figures they've given up,' he murmured.

Now O'Keefe was joined by Oscar Sheppard. Olds's widow, who had retreated into a world of her own, stayed where she was, curled up in the corner where her husband lay dead beneath an old, stained blanket.

Long moments passed as they watched Billy take one cautious step, then another, then half a dozen. Finally, he stood still among the bodies of men and mounts, and looked around. The silence was heavy, absolute, as each man watching braced himself for the inevitable gun blast that would tear Billy off his feet and signal a new and possibly final attack.

But no gun blast came. His appearance there in the grounds of Adobe Walls provoked no reaction at all from anyone who might be out there, watching for them.

Another taut thirty seconds passed, and at last Billy broke his silence. '*It's over!*' he yelled, and even from this distance Hennessy caught the barely suppressed sob in his voice. '*They've gone!*'

Hennessy thought he heard a tired cheer go up from the men in the saloon. For sure he heard his own companions muttering behind him, their voices tinged with a mixture of puzzlement and disbelief.

Gone? No, it's a trick, it's gotta be. . . .

He pushed up on tired, stiff muscles, went to the big double doorway, lifted the bar and went out into the harsh morning light, squinting a little. Billy saw him, came trotting over as battle-weary men began to emerge from saloon and store alike.

'It's over, Cal!' Billy called, his bloodshot, light-starved eyes narrowed against the sun. When he was near enough, he clapped Hennessy on one arm. 'By God, we taught them heathens a lesson, didn't we?'

'I'd say they taught *us* one,' Hennessy replied mildly.

Billy's whiskery face clouded as he remembered the dead. He drew a breath, let it go in a soft sigh. 'Well, they've gone. And we survived it. I reckon that's all that matters now.'

Hennessy was about to agree when he glanced over Billy's right shoulder and felt something in his pale blue eyes die. He swallowed, said softly, 'I don't think it *is* over, Billy.'

Billy read the look in his face and wheeled around with sudden urgency. There on a far distant ridge sat a small number of mounted Indians, fanned out in a ragged line, maybe as many as fifteen.

He swore, and his shoulders sagged visibly. They hadn't gone, then. They were still out there, watching. waiting, plotting. . . .

The strangled sound Billy made came from someplace deep inside his chest. His fists clenched, his shoulders bunched again, he glared at the distant war-party with teeth clenched and his every muscle suddenly locked tightly into place. Then whatever it was that held him there broke, and he looked around, saw Hanrahan standing nearby and started over to him, his stride fast, purposeful.

'Jimmy!' he barked, holding out his hands, 'gimme that rifle.'

Hanrahan frowned. 'Billy—'

'Gimme that damn' rifle!' growled Billy, snatching the Sharps .50/.90 from the startled saloon-man's grasp.

Hennessy followed him over. 'Whoa, Billy!' he said. 'What do you suppose you can do from here? That ridge is about a mile away!'

Billy turned on him. His face was heated now, his normally mild, good-humoured eyes round and a little wild. 'What can I hope to do?' he grated. 'I'll *show* you what I'm gonna do! I'm gonna show them red bastards that they messed with the wrong crew here!'

And so saying, he slapped the stock of the heavy buffalo gun to his right cheek and took aim.

This was not the way it should have gone. Their attack on the white man's stockade should have been short and decisive, a complete and bloodless victory for Quanah and his allies.

But here they were, three days later, and the stockade still stood, was still in the hands of the whites, and Isatai's promises of invulnerability had proved to be worthless.

Quanah, himself wounded, was no longer prepared to indulge the shaman. He simply could not accept that so many braves had doubted the Sacred Powers and been punished for it. And neither did those around him. In any case, the facts spoke for themselves. So far, upwards of seventy braves had died in this contest. *Seventy*! And still a mere handful of whites prevailed against a force of hundreds.

Quanah sat his horse on a rise overlooking Adobe Walls. At this distance, the stockade looked tiny, inconsequential. Sitting their mounts alongside him were Satanta and Lone Wolf, Stone Calf, Grey Beard, Mow-way, Wild Horse and others, all equally disappointed, equally angry, equally sceptical now of Isatai.

For his part, the medicine man faced them from beneath lowered brows, feeling their fury and mistrust, and trying hard to curb his own growing self-doubt.

'So,' said Quanah, breaking the early morning silence. 'What have you to say for yourself, Isatai? Or do you *have* no explanations?'

Isatai was about to respond when a scar-faced Comanche, unable to maintain his place in the ranks behind them any longer, suddenly ran forward, his right cheek twisted by an old bullet wound that had healed to form a livid spider-shape. The brave was heavy-set, about forty or so, and clearly tormented.

'He has no answers!' he cried. 'You know, Quanah, you know that no one had a stronger belief in the Sacred Powers than my son, my beloved Tahkay! And yet he now lies cold and dead down there! And for what? Will Isatai tell us that the gods made a mistake? Or is the only mistake *ours*, in that we ever trusted his assurances at all?'

Quanah turned his attention back to Isatai, who seemed to wilt beneath his burning gaze. 'What do you say to that, holy one?'

Isatai, the hollow-eyed living skeleton, drew himself up only with effort. 'Sometimes the gods feel it is necessary to test us,' he began.

But that was as far as he got. Tahkay's father suddenly screamed out, stiffened, then spun around and fell to the ground, clutching at a shallow, bloody furrow in his back.

155

A second later, they all heard the distant boom of a heavy-calibre rifle.

The assembled chiefs fought to bring their startled horses under control. For a moment spooked animals swapped ends, back-stepped and bumped into each other. When order began to return, Satanta stared at the distant stockade, now populated by a gathering of ant-sized figures, and asked, 'What magic is this?'

Lone Wolf shared his unease. 'How can we fight men who can so easily harm us from such a distance?'

Gamely, Isatai gestured at the fallen man, who was now slowly climbing back to his feet, and said, 'This man spoke out of turn, and the gods chose to punish him for—'

All at once Quahah was a rush of movement. He heeled his horse forward and lashed out, silencing the shaman with a furious back-hand slap. The red blood that trickled from Isatai's split lip contrasted starkly to the yellow paint in which he was covered.

'No more of your lies!' Quanah hissed. He pulled an Army Colt from his sash and stabbed it into the other man's face, thumb-cocking the hammer as he did so. The other chieftains watched on, eyes lit with approval and anticipation.

But a moment later Quanah let the gun drop from Isatai's fear-frozen face and he shook his head in disgust.

'Where is the justice in sparing you the fate you so richly deserve?' he asked quietly. 'Go from this place, Isatai. Go and be forever shunned, for the story of your lies will go ahead of you, and you will be spurned by all.

156

'*That* is your punishment, holy man – not a quick and merciful death, but the long and lonely life of an outcast, exposed for the liar and trickster you are, and justly despised for it!'

Mouth agape, Isatai looked around, found Eagle Hand among the warriors crowded behind them and raised his eyebrows. Eagle Hand, once his biggest admirer, shook his head and spat off to one side. Clearly he could expect no support from that quarter. No support from any quarter.

'But I proved it to you,' he said, returning his attention to Quanah. 'The bullet Eagle Hand fired at me—'

'—was most likely emptied of all but enough powder to make it fly from the gun that fired it,' Quanah snapped with a sudden flash of insight. 'Another ruse to lend credence to your claims.'

He sighed, suddenly tired beyond belief. 'Go now, Isatai. Find a place in which to live out the remainder of your life in peace . . . if you can. And as for the rest of us. . . .' He hesitated, glanced to left and right, at his fellow chieftains. 'There will be other battles, my brothers. But there will be no more fighting here. Here, we are finished. Here,' he whispered bitterly, 'it is over.'

Two days after the Indians pulled out, a mixed force of some one hundred men, alerted by Shaun Millican's dramatic arrival in Dodge, galloped into Adobe Walls. They were eager for a fight, but found the fighting over – at least for now.

Instead they found the survivors of what would go down in history as the Battle of Adobe Walls getting ready to quit the stockade for good. The arrival of the buffalo hunters in these parts had lit the fuse to the Indians' anger. But the explosion, the *real* explosion, was still to come. They didn't care to be around when that finally occurred.

Hennessy stood out front of the bullet-scarred saloon, in the sunshine of the new day, and checked his cinch. Billy stood to one side, watching him prepare to pull out. Around them the other buffalo hunters were all of the same mind. Teams were being hitched to surviving or repaired wagons loaded down with skins, and hunters were packing their belongings away before beginning the long journey back to Dodge.

'A sad day,' said Billy. 'Hate like hell to turn my back on such rich pickin's, and I suspect the rest of these boys feel much the same way.'

Hennessy nodded, until his pale blue eyes happened to fall on a single, lonely figure standing, head bent, outside the eatery. Such was the pain and bewilderment in Mrs Olds that he could almost feel it himself, even from this distance.

'Not everyone'll be sorry to see the back of this place,' he noted.

Billy nodded soberly. 'Yup,' he agreed. 'There's more'n a few who've lost just about ever'thin' from this business.'

'Well, you'll get over it,' Hennessy said encouragingly. 'You and all these other fellers'll head for Kansas or Colorado or the Panhandle and start up again, and before you know it, it'll be business as usual.'

158

'And the Indians?'

'They'll be right behind you, Billy, waiting to finish what they started here.'

He took one final look at Adobe Walls and shook his head. 'This way of life's more or less finished, Billy. There's not the demand there used to be, and nowhere near the money to be made. Sooner or later you men'll have to start looking for a new line of work.'

'Got any suggestions?'

'As a matter of fact. . . .'

'Go on.'

'Cattle,' said Hennessy. 'Think about it. You've more or less starved the Indians out of these parts and pretty near finished off the buffalo doing it. That leaves a hell of a lot of range open for the taking, and it's the cattle-men who'll claim it.'

'You sayin' I ought to go push cows for a livin'?'

'That's for you to decide. But even that's a better way to live than the one you've been following.'

Billy considered that for a while. At length he said, 'You fancy comin' along for the experience?'

'Not me, Billy. I'm too damn' fiddle-footed to stay in any one place for long. There's a lot of country out there, and I aim to see as much of it as I can. But maybe Masterson and Sheppard would care to give it a whirl.' He spotted the Newfoundland dog sitting beside the fire-blackened wreckage of the Scheidler wagon. 'Take that crazy hound with you,' he said. 'He could use a new owner.'

Billy nodded thoughtfully, then offered his hand. 'Well, I won't say it's been a pleasure, exactly, but it's

been good to see you again, Cal. For all your damn'
sermonizin'.'

Hennessy smiled at him. 'I'll see you again sometime,' he promised as he swung into the saddle. 'Next
time I figure your conscience needs a little pricking,
maybe.'

As he gathered up the reins, he felt a curious sense
of sadness coupled with relief. Relief that what had
happened here was over, sadness that it had ever had
come to this in the first place.

Still, it would be a long time before the buffalo in
these parts heard the chilling thunder of a Big Fifty
again. For now, at least, the slaughter of man and beast
was over. And if it came to that, so too was the brief
moment in history when white men had dared to
invade *Comancheria* and call this place east of the Santa
Fe Trail and south of the Canadian River *home.*